Scooter

Cerberus MC Book 11
Marie James

Copyright

Scooter: Cerberus MC Book 11
Copyright © 2019 Marie James
Editing by Marie James Betas

Acknowledgments

Huge shout out this time around to the #1 man in my life! My dear, sweet husband, you are amazing! Thank you for making my dreams come true and supporting me relentlessly from day one. This wouldn't be possible it is wasn't for your support!

My amazing BETAs, you ladies are the absolute best! Laura, MaRanda, Brenda, Jamie, Michelle, and Jo thank you so much for the help on this book! Mary, you amaze me each and every time we work together! Thank you for your help and all of your support through this process!

Laura Watson! Thank you! You keep my head on right. I couldn't do this without you!

Another shout out to RRR Promotions and Natasha for helping get this book out into the world. As always you nailed it!
A million thank yous to Wildfire PR for helping get this together.

Readers, I can't even begin to tell you what you mean to me. Without you, I'd have no reason to write these books. Thanks for your continued support of the Cerberus MC!

Until next time!
~Marie James

Synopsis:

I'm no one's savior.

I work with the Cerberus MC for the thrills, not for the glory.

Saving people who've been trafficked is just a side benefit, coming in second to the adrenaline rush of eradicating some of the evil in the world.

Mia Vazquez didn't seem to get the memo.

When I pulled her out of Hell, she wouldn't let go. She literally wrapped her arms around my neck and refused to release me.

I did the only thing I could do; I held her back.

For weeks I stayed by her side, comforting her and assuring her things would eventually get better.

She managed to climb inside of me, and then she took off.

Mia Vazquez didn't get the memo.

She's mine, and letting go of me doesn't mean I'll let go of her.

Prologue

Scooter

This mission is personal.

I hate when shit gets personal.

I love my job, and I love working for Cerberus, but things get squirrelly when emotions are involved.

Emotions complicate everything. They leave room for mistakes, and since my ass is on the line this morning, it's making me itchy. Today has to go well, not just for me and the other men putting their lives in danger to shut down Luis Jiménez but also for the women he's entrapped in his Miami compound.

So, I do my best to get my head in the game. This can't be personal for me. This is just another mission to help rid the world of some piece of shit scum who thinks he rules the world with no oversight.

He took the wrong girl this time, and for Max Vazquez, it's personal. His sister is thought to be inside, and as Max looks on from the command center a few miles away, we breach the compound.

This is a mission like every one before it, I remind myself as I follow behind Jinx.

This isn't personal for me. I've let that thought run through my head over and over. Dead girls in places like this aren't uncommon, and even though everyone is holding out hope that today's invasion is different, we all know in the backs of our minds that there's a good chance Mia Vazquez will be added to the body count.

She's been gone for seven weeks, and it doesn't take long for men like Jiménez and his crew to ruin the women they abduct. These girls are used up and replaced like a carton of milk in a preschool.

"Forty-five seconds," Shadow says. "Godspeed, guys."

The familiar voice in my ear steadies me, and my mind goes blank, only leaving room for the main objective.

My trigger finger twitches, anxious to engage, but doing so prematurely would only lead to havoc.

We're on the first four guards at the entrance before their brains can register we're there, and they go down with barely a whoosh of air as their villainous lives are snuffed out.

Like alley cats searching for prey, we make our way closer to the compound. I fan out with Jinx, Rocker, and Hound as the other guys split off to the other side of the compound. We studied the schematics of this place with laser focus, and we all have our goals.

Taking down the semi-automatic-toting guards is child's play as we split again. Jinx and Hound head into the rooms they're responsible for, and I clear mine.

More shots ring out around me, but by this point in my career, they don't even phase me. Unless I get hit, those noises aren't my concern.

"What the fuck?" Jinx hisses.

Another shot echoes through the compound, this one closer, heard with my own ears rather than through the mic.

"He was fucking a gash in her side," Jinx says.

"That was Miguel 'Toro' Montoya," Shadow says into his mic from the command room. "Keep moving, Jinx."

"Sick fuck," I mutter as I delve deeper through the compound.

A guy, too drunk to be carrying a weapon, stumbles out into the hallway, but I drop him before he can raise his rifle.

"Piece of shit," I mutter as I put another bullet between his eyes and step over his body.

Like most jobs we're tasked with, there's a kill order on every man in this place. If they even look at us wrong, we're ordered to drop them. So, unless they're literally on their knees waving a little white flag, they're as good as dead, and even with surrender, my finger might slip on the trigger. None of these guys deserve to live.

I move silently, coming close to Rocker as he trains his gun down the hall in front of me. I release a low whistle, so he knows who's behind him, but before he can acknowledge me, he goes down.

"Rocker's hit," I report into my mic without so much as a hint of emotion.

"Report," Shadow demands.

"H-hit my vest," Rocker wheezes.

"Lie low, Rocker. Let them finish this, and then we can get you out of there," Shadow instructs.

A whistle sounds out from behind me just as three guys round the corner. Without aim or care where they're shooting, the hallway is sprayed with bullets, but Jinx and I are low, prepared for the idiots, and they fall just as hard as the scumbags before them.

"Clear," Hound reports, and Jinx and I do the same.

"Guess you're buying the drinks tonight," I tell Rocker as I lean down to inspect the lead in his vest.

He chuckles on another wheeze and smiles.

"Asshole," he grunts. "Get my ass out of here."

"Come on, man," Jinx says as he joins us, holding out his hand for Rocker to clasp.

Jinx and Rocker head back toward the front as I nudge open the last door in the hall. I have two Cerberus guys at my back as we enter, probably Hound and Grinch going by our entry points.

The air in the room is stagnant and filled with the tangy scent of fear.

No less than a dozen women are huddled together against the far wall. Like usual, they don't squeal or scream, and it only lends to the fact that they have been tortured and beaten down for so long that even though they're scared, the end doesn't seem as daunting as it may have been the first time men rushed into this room.

I search the room, letting my eyes roam over each and every one of them. My vision isn't hampered in the dark room due to my night vision, but it's times like this that I wish I couldn't see at all. Shaking with fear, yet not making a noise, the women are covered in cuts, bruises, and clear evidence of their abuse.

"Mia?" I say softly, looking toward a woman who has silent tears running down her face.

She's filthy and trembling, holding a bandaged arm against her chest as she cowers further, no doubt praying that the floor will open up and transport her someplace else.

"Scooter, do you have her?" Shadow asks.

"Mia Vazquez?" I ask as I bend down closer to her.

Although her features are the same, she looks like a ghost of the woman in the picture we were given before we got started tonight. She's thinner, easily twenty pounds lighter, and the long, dark hair I stared at a little too long is tangled, and patches are missing. Dead eyes look back at me, and the poor girl is so filthy, she looks like she was forced to run through a muddy field.

"I'm going to pick you up, Mia," I tell her as I sling my rifle around to my back and reach out for her.

She doesn't freeze up or recoil when I lift her in my arms, but she doesn't cling to me either. She's dead weight in my arms as I carry her from Hell, weighing less than a sack of feathers.

"I'm Ryan Gabhart," I begin, hoping that my voice is calming. "I work for the Cerberus MC out of New Mexico. I'm thirty-four. I spent ten years in the Marine Corps before coming to work for these guys."

I walk slowly, tucking her head against my chest as we pass the dead men in the hallway.

"I'm an only child. I hate pineapple on pizza, and I think men who hurt women should all die slow painful deaths."

She wraps her arm around my neck and buries herself deeper into my chest. And for some reason, I do something I've never done while carrying a broken woman to safety—I hold her tighter and I'm reluctant to let her go when we reach the medics outside.

Chapter 1

Scooter

Waiting at the hospital as each woman is seen by medical staff and treated is the part I hate the most. It's nearly impossible to keep your distance from what happened to them when it's right in your face for hours afterward.

"You gonna live?" I ask Rocker when he hobbles into the waiting room from being seen himself.

He flips up his middle finger before falling unceremoniously into the chair beside me.

"Getting shot always fucking sucks," he grumbles as he moves and groans, unable to find a comfortable position.

"That's why I always aim not to get shot." He huffs an incredulous laugh. "How many did you take?"

"Three," he answers. "All center mass."

"Thank fuck for top of the line Kevlar, am I right?"

We fist bump, and he gives me a weak smile. Joking about getting shot is the only thing we can do. If we focus on the fact that if the shithead's aim was a mere six inches higher, Rocker would be laid out on a slab in the morgue, we'd lose our minds. The fear would seep into us like cancer, making it impossible to continue doing what we do. I've seen great men succumb to the terror of getting killed while executing these types of jobs, and honestly, we're all just one wicked thought away from it happening to us.

That's why Cerberus only recruits the best of the best. All members were once active Marines in their prime with commendations from their commanders and the ability to look death in the face and smile.

That's why sitting in the hospital waiting room is the worst part. These women give names and faces to the brutality we're fighting against. It makes it dangerous for us.

"Fuck," I grumble as I stand.

Rocker just chuckles as I walk away. He's one of my closest friends in Cerberus, and he knows how this part makes me antsy.

I roam the hospital, still geared up in combat gear minus the weapons. Nurses and doctors alike stare as I walk past them, but no one opens their mouths to tell me I need a pass or permission to travel the halls. Many stop and thank me for what we did today, and I merely answer them with a grunt and quick nod. I don't do this for the praise, and even though it makes me an asshole, I didn't join Cerberus with a clear focus on ridding the world of pieces of shit. I'm in it for the adrenaline rush and the thrill of the job. The women we rescue are just a bonus; the cherry on top of the adventure. At least for me it's always been that way.

Shouts echo around me, and instead of standing there and watching the drama unfold like numerous people I pass, I head straight for the action.

The screams get louder as I approach, and it isn't until I'm standing in the doorway that I realize I'm in Mia Vazquez's room. Max is sitting beside the bed, his mother and father clinging to each other as they both cry. A man I don't recognize looks torn between going to her and running the hell away.

Mia is so tiny on the hospital bed. Covered in bruises with a new dressing on her broken arm, she screams as she tries to ball herself up.

"What the fuck?" I hiss as I push inside of the room.

Her head snaps in my direction and dark brown eyes look over me, assessing as if she's trying to figure out who I am and if I'm another threat she's perceived.

Her pupils dilate the second she recognizes me, and even though she's screaming at her family as if they're the devil incarnate, her wails stop as she reaches out for me. I don't know why I close the distance between us. Maybe it's her quivering chin or the utter devastation in her eyes, but before my brain can register the action, I'm at her bedside.

"Shh, Mia. I got you," I whisper as I climb into the bed with her.

I'm cautious of the wires and cords monitoring her vitals as I pull her to my chest. She fastens herself to me like our time is limited and I'm going to disappear if she blinks her eyes.

"Do they know each other?" the unfamiliar man snaps.

My jaw clenches with his questions, and if I wasn't trying to stop this poor, broken girl from trembling, I'd snap his head back with the impact of my damn fist.

"Yes," Tug whispers. "He's her savior."

I want to roll my eyes and tell everyone in this damn room that I'm no one's savior, but Mia's tiny fists cling to my shirt, and she becomes my only focus.

She's cleaner now than she was hours ago, but the noxious scent from being held in captivity for so long still lingers in the air. In the better lighting, it's clear part of her abuse included the destruction of her gorgeous hair, and even though there are chunks missing where it was sheared down to her scalp, I run a calming hand over her head and down her back. I do this over and over until her wailing softens to hiccupping sobs.

"I like the mountains more than anything else," I whisper to her, knowing that she can hear my low voice. I ignore the tears wetting my clothes and hold her tighter. "I like to hike and ski, but a nice calm beach has its place as well."

"Can someone please tell me what's going on?" the stranger whisper-hisses.

I don't even lift my head. I press my mouth to Mia's head and continue to whisper mundane details about my life.

"Has she been having an affair with that man?"

It's takes everything I have not to chuckle with the ridiculous question. This woman was abducted seven weeks ago, held in what could be considered a dungeon, and had God only knows what happen to her, and this asshole is worried that she's having an affair? Some men are complete idiots, and this one is clearly a selfish twat who has no business even being in the room.

"That's it," I hear Max hiss, but instead of a fist meeting the douche's face, Tug drags the jerk out of the room by the collar of his shirt.

I keep my lips moving, telling Mia about my life back home in Indiana but keep my ears open in an attempt to hear what's being said in the hallway.

He's livid as evident from his tone, but then the word fiancé filters to me, and I kind of feel sorry for the schmuck. I'd be livid if my girl was wrapped around another man, but if he was who she wanted right now, she would've reached for him instead of me.

I've seen this happen in the field. In the Middle East, although uncommon, sometimes, the women of the village would attach themselves to the military guys. Although most women kept their distance, mainly because of religious reasons and upbringing, some saw the soldiers as their only hope for freedom or escape from the lives they were born into.

But that's in a land filled with oppression and limited means. We're in Florida for fuck's sake. Mia has her brother and both of her parents here to lean on. Hell, her fiancé is throwing a fit in the hall because he wants to be the man she leans on for comfort. Yet here she is, snuggled in my arms and finally breathing evenly.

We have a debriefing in ten minutes, but I can't seem to pull myself from her bed. Each time I shift my weight, she whimpers and holds on to me tighter.

An hour passes, and I'm reluctant to leave, but we're pulling out and leaving Miami in fifteen minutes. In a deep enough sleep that her arms fall away from me when I stand, I press my lips to Mia's forehead and whisper encouraging words to her. She's asleep, but with any luck they'll seep into her consciousness and ease some of her suffering.

Without a word, I nod to her parents and leave the room.

Max catches me in the hall, shaking my hand and thanking me for helping his sister. Even though it's out of character for me, I offer him my phone number and let him add his into my contacts, telling him that if he needs anything else, not to hesitate to reach out. It's more of a placation than anything. His sister will heal eventually, even though I know it's going to be a long, uphill battle.

I can finally take a deep breath when the front doors of the hospital open with a whoosh, and I step outside. I'm fifteen feet from the freedom of the SUVs when my phone chirps a text. Normally, I'd ignore it until we're on the road, but with the sound comes an uneasy feeling that settles in my gut, and when I pull my phone from my pocket, that instinct is confirmed.

Max: She needs you, man. She woke up screaming again.

I lift my eyes to the guys waiting for me, finding Kincaid's. He must have heard what happened in Mia's room during the debriefing with the other guys because he gives me a nod, and it's all that I need to turn back around.

My parents will be sad I won't make Christmas, but there's something more important that I have to take care of. I don't feel an ounce of irritation as I head back into the hospital, and the guys pull away from the curb.

Leaving her bed was harder than it was to pass her off to the medics back at the compound, but it's the knowledge that each time I have to walk away from her will only be harder makes me slow my steps as I close the distance between me and her room.

I vow to give her a week tops before I explain that I have a life to get back to.

What I don't anticipate is feeling like a week with her will never be enough.

Chapter 2

Mia

Closing my eyes is the worst.

When I'm no longer able to resist and sleep takes over is when the demons return.

It's when I'm thrown back into the nightmare, I feel like I'll never be able to rid myself of completely.

It's when the hands and sneering faces of my captors once again get ahold of me.

It's when the smells and the sounds of the whimpering women infiltrate my head.

It's the destruction of my body, my mind, and my soul.

I jolt awake before the man with the scars on his face can drag me back to his lair, and I wake up in the warm and protective arms of Ryan. He's the only one who makes the fear manageable. He's the only one I want near me. And even though I question my sanity for clinging to this stranger, he's the only person who quiets the screams and the terror coursing through my head.

It's all coming to an end today. I've heard my parents and my dead brother speaking about my discharge. The thought of Ryan leaving my side frightens me more than the car ride I took seven weeks ago with my head covered in a cloth bag so thick my own breaths were stifled until I thought I'd die of asphyxiation.

Max isn't supposed to be here, and yet his presence is a constant reminder that nothing makes sense anymore. He speaks to me, reminding me of all the things I lost when my twin died in a car accident a decade ago. His death, the loss of half of who I am, was a blow I never thought I'd recover from. And even though he's said the words, even though he whispered the entire story of what happened ten years ago, I still can't let myself believe that he's really here.

Men don't come back from the dead, a fact I've repeated over and over in my head since Ryan told me all of the men at the compound were now worm food. They haunt me in my nightmares, but they can no longer hurt me while I'm awake. It's a small consolation for what has happened since I decided to make a quick stop at the mall on my way home from work.

That day plays on repeat even when I try my hardest to think of anything else.

I've tried to change the scenario in my mind. I walk away from the smiling handsome guy in the parking lot rather than speak to him about my car trouble. I refuse his offer of help when he winks at me with a dangerous smirk.

Hell, I even recreate my home life, trying to convince myself that Jason was around more often rather than spending all of his free time at the office, so I wasn't enthralled with the good-looking guy because I had a doting fiancé waiting for me.

But it always ends the same. I still walk to his car so he can get a jack for my flat tire. I still end up with a bag over my head and rough hands on my back as he tied me up and shoved me in the trunk. I still end up at the mercy of men who don't listen to the word no. I still end up being used, hurt, and vowed to that I'll never see my family or the light of day ever again.

I believed those men because they made promises that they kept. They told me that they'd hurt me, and they did. They told me that I'd never be the same, and I know that's as true as I know that I'm leaving here today whether I want to or not. They told me I'd die in that compound, and even though I'm on the other side of their torment, I know I'm dead.

I feel it bone-deep, the emptiness and despair.

I feel the pain and degradation of what happened to my body against my will.

I feel cold and indifferent to what happens next. I'm buried under my racing thoughts and inability to heal on the inside.

But even though I don't care what happened because I've suffered things no person should, I still hold on to Ryan like he's my buoy in a sea of doubt and anguish. He's the only thing keeping me rooted to the here and now. It's not my mother or father, not the specter of my twin coming back to life, and it surely isn't Jason, whom I haven't seen since I woke up from surgery days ago.

I blink my eyes open, visually verifying that my anchor is still at my side even though I can feel the warmth of his body against mine.

The people around me talk as if I'm not there, and I know it's because they think I'm so lost in my head that I'm not paying attention, but vigilance is the only reason they didn't pull my body, dead and rotting, from the compound. Giving up now seems like the best idea, but while there, all I wanted was to be free. All I wanted was the do-over that I was never afforded while I was their toy to play with and abuse. The undertaking seems like too much work, so I hold on to him harder and bury my nose in his shirt.

His hand, the same one that reached for me while I cowered in that dark room, runs the length of my back, and it's comforting, but it's his words, his simple tales of childhood and every minute detail of his life before today that calms me. I know more about Ryan Gabhart, *Scooter* to his MC friends, than I do about my own fiancé, and that's telling.

"They're going to release you today, Mia," Ryan whispers as my parents and Max argue over what happens next.

I hold him tighter, refusing to acknowledge the pain in my broken arm. It's nothing compared to the dread settling over me at the thought of not having him.

"She's coming home with us," Pa declares. "It's where she needs to be."

Home is where I was abducted. If I never step foot on Louisiana soil again in my life, it'll be too soon.

"Mia?" Ryan nudges my head with his shoulder, but I refuse to lift it.

I haven't said a word to him; not one single phrase has left my mouth since seeing the halo of light around him as he lifted me from the floor and carried me to safety. It hasn't, however, kept him from speaking to me like he hasn't been carrying on a one-sided conversation for days.

"Mia?" He nudges me again, and I know if I don't look up at him, he's only going to continue to do the very same thing until I give him my attention. What the man doesn't know is that he's had my undivided attention all along.

I take in the dark scruff on his face. It's only grown thicker as he stayed by my side constantly. Tattoos peek out from the V-neck of his t-shirt, and although I'm curious, it's his dark eyes peering down at me that garners all of my attention. They're filled with a sincerity I've never seen before, and it's what I focused on when he and his team came into that room. The gear and guns should've scared me, and at first they did, but then he crouched low and spoke my name, and I swore he was some sort avenging angel sent to emancipate me from Hell.

And he did all of that and more. I know he doesn't have to sit with me. He could've easily ignored me when I reached for him that first time. He could've let the doctors sedate me like they were discussing when I reached for him again only moments after waking to find him gone.

"They're going to discharge you this afternoon," he repeats, his voice calming and soft. "Do you understand?"

I nod, knowing what's going to happen and hating the world for it.

"Your parents want you to go home."

My eyes dart across the room finding my dad holding onto my sobbing mother. I think she's cried more tears since I woke up than I did the entire time I was gone, and that's saying a lot since my face was constantly wet.

"Is that what you want?"

My head shakes violently.

"Where do you want to go?"

I cling to him again, but he nudges my chin with his strong hand when I try to bury my face in his chest.

"Where, Mia? Where will you feel safe?"

My throat is drier than I realize when I open my mouth to speak. It takes a few tries before I'm able to speak. Short of my screaming fits a few days ago; I haven't spoken at all.

"With you," I finally manage. "I want to be with you."

Silence fills the room, but I don't have to look at my family to know they are staring at me. Sensing eyes on me was one of the first skills I honed after being abducted. Drawing attention to yourself always meant bad news, and even now, in the safety of his arms and under the scrutiny of his dark eyes, terror once again fills my blood. My heart begins to race, and I'm thankful that the monitors have been removed because otherwise everyone in this room would know how scared I was becoming. They'd see my weakness and use it against me.

"Shh," Ryan coos as he places his warm palm on my neck and urges me against his chest. I go willingly, knowing that I'm safe in the cocoon of his arms.

"That's not going to happen," Max hisses after a long silent moment.

"She needs to be with her family," Pa adds.

"I can take care of her," Ma says on another sob.

I love my mother dearly, and I know her heart is in the right place even though it's broken into tiny shreds, but the incessant crying is driving me up the wall. She doesn't have a clear picture of what happened to me, and I never want her to, but I listened to constant crying for weeks. Every day was filled with the tears and pleas of broken women who had no other recourse to survival other than weeping the time away. I've had more than enough of it.

The tremors start in my hands and before long, they've made their way into my arms and down my spine until my body is shaking uncontrollably. My teeth chatter as if I'm stuck in the tundra with nothing to protect my skin from the freezing temps, and I doubt I'll ever be warm again.

"Jason misses her and is expecting her home," Ma whispers.

"Fuck him," Max spits, and if I weren't a shivering mess, I might have smiled at his outburst.

I don't miss Jason at all. I don't miss his arms around me or the huge rock he put on my finger months ago. I don't miss the way he'd parade me around his friends and at parties, showing me off like a prized cow rather than the love of his life. Before he even proposed, I had begun to feel like I was just another steppingstone, just another expectation from his bosses at the law firm he's been trying to make partner at for the last three years. Established men in law were supposed to be married and having a couple of kids to pose for the Christmas card were an added bonus.

"She's going to New Mexico."

"Abso-fucking-lutely not!" Max yells. "She needs to be home with her family."

"You want to talk about what your family needs?" Ryan seethes, but I hear his jaw snap forcibly shut when I twist his shirt in my hand. "It's not a discussion. It's what she wants."

Chapter 3

Scooter

"You're going to love New Mexico," I tell Mia as we load into the shuttle. "The weatherman is predicting a dusting of snow later this week. I know that's probably hard to think about considering it's over seventy degrees here in Florida, but we'll need to grab you a jacket at the airport."

Her brother rolls his eyes before focusing out the window.

For all the protesting Max did at the hospital, he hasn't said a negative word since we left yesterday. He didn't even complain about sleeping on the couch in the hotel room we got last night a mile from the airport when we discovered that all flights to New Mexico were full. It didn't keep his eyes from glaring at me when I climbed in bed with Mia and let her wrap herself around me.

One snide comment about that shit and I would've knocked his damn head off. The man doesn't know me, but he's well aware of the reputation of the Cerberus men. He should know that I don't take what's going on with Mia lightly, and even though she's still gorgeous even with her broken arm and bruise-covered face, I'm not an opportunist willing to compromise her mental health for a little grinding.

Even though there will be nothing more between Mia and me than offering her the comfort she only seems to find with me, I'm not bitter or even agitated with her neediness. I feel inadequate most days when even my arms around her doesn't seem to be enough to keep the nightmares at bay.

Last night was worse rather than better as I'd hoped. I figured the quiet would soothe her, but the room is darker, and the lack of activity just made it easier to hear the sporadic noises that accompany a hotel. I would've gotten the presidential suite at the most expensive hotel in town if I thought it would ease her even a little.

She refused the clothes her mother brought her, and she somehow ended up in my sleep pants and t-shirt. I offered to stand guard outside of the bathroom door while she showered because she began shaking like a leaf again when I suggested the warm water would feel amazing. She dragged me inside the bathroom and locked the door, so I stood with my back to her, steam filling the room as she took a three-minute shower. Thank fuck, Max had left to go grab food because I probably would've gotten my ass kicked for that.

Warmer than I'm used to air hits us in the face when we climb out of the shuttle. Max hovers near his sister, but she stays at my side. I know it grates on him that he's not the one she's leaning on, but he needs to realize that she was abducted thinking he'd been dead for the last ten years. So not only does she have to deal with what happened while she was here, but she also has to wrap her head around the fact that her twin is back amongst the living. Just that alone is enough to make nearly any sane person crazy.

As I expected, the Miami International Airport is swarmed with people. It's the day after Christmas and thousands of people are already over the holidays and ready to get back home.

"Maybe we can get you a pretzel," I tell her as I urge her toward the security checkpoint. "One of those ones that are crunchy on the outside and all warm and gooey on the inside. I love mine with spicy mustard, but they never seem to have the right kind at the airport."

I turn her to face me when her eyes widen at a scruffy man standing in line in front of her. I reposition us so my back is to him, and hers is to Max. She's wary of her brother but hasn't shown any signs of being terrified of him.

"What do you think?" I continue, even though I know she isn't going to answer me. For some reason, my voice seems to calm her, and I'll talk all day long for a hundred years if it keeps her from being afraid. "Maybe you prefer ice cream or one of those two-thousand-calorie cinnamon rolls that taste like heaven but are so bad for you, they have to have been created by the devil himself?"

"She likes French fries," Max interjects, but Mia frowns when he speaks.

"French fries?" I smile at Mia, tossing Max a fucking bone I don't think he deserves. "We have this cilantro-lime aioli back at the clubhouse that is amazing with French fries, but you have to try it with those huge potato wedges, not those scrimpy little fries. You'll love it."

My heart nearly beats out of my chest when I see a tiny smile tug up the right corner of her mouth. It's gone in the blink of an eye, but it was there. It's the first sign of life other than her tears and the trembling of her body when I'm more than a few feet away from her.

Max nods his head indicating that it's our turn to drop our belongings in the bins and walk through the x-ray machine. Mia's fingers begin to tap on her legs, and I know she's seconds away from freaking out.

"You've flown before, right? This is no different. We're going to show our IDs to the gate agent, and then I'm going to go through first. Max will be right behind you. I know he seems a little wimpy compared to me, but he'd never let anyone hurt you. Three minutes tops, and then you're right by my side. Okay?" I dip lower, forcing her to look me in the eye rather than past me to the conveyor belt waiting for our things.

She doesn't speak, but her spine stiffens as she stands up a little straighter, and I take that as her being able to do this. My own nervousness grows as we wait for the belt to clear enough for me to toss my duffel bag up there. I help Mia with her shoes when she makes no effort to take them off herself, before clasping her hand and promising her all sorts of fun and adventures when we get to New Mexico. I keep my eyes on her as I lift my arms to be scanned in the machine and wait impatiently as she follows behind me and does the same.

Her dark eyes search my face as the machine spins around her, but in a matter of seconds, it's over, and the TSA agent manning the equipment shuffles her through. I grab her hand and pull her to my chest the second she's done. Her pulse pounds erratically against my fingers as I press them to her wrist, but we're not out of the woods yet. By the grace of God alone, my bag doesn't get dinged but seeing as I shipped home a ton of shit yesterday, I was hoping it wouldn't. We carry a ridiculous amount of things with us when we head out for work, and not even a third of it would be allowed on a commercial flight, hence the reason we take the Cerberus jet.

Mia is a trembling mess by the time I crouch again to help her with her shoes, and her unease doesn't go unnoticed. People stare, whispering to their traveling companions, and I expected this as well. They don't see her as a survivor like Max and I do. They only see the arm in a cast and the dozens of bruises marking her pretty face. People sneer at both of us, no doubt in their narrow minds thinking we're the ones responsible for her injuries.

By the time we make it to our gate, Mia is in a state of utter terror, so I do the only thing I know will work. I find us as quiet a corner as I can, and I pull her onto my lap. Max doesn't say a word. He's well aware by now how much it calms her, so he stands sentry over us while I cradle her in my arms and remind her of all the things she'll see when we get to the clubhouse.

By the time we board, she's calmer, but it doesn't last long as the guy who scared her in line is also on our flight and a mere eight feet away across the aisle. I situate my huge body in the center seat, lifting the armrest between so she can settle against my chest. Her tiny frame nearly folds in on itself as she brings her knees to her chest and leans against me. I wrap my arms all the way around her, legs and all, and tell her about the time I got caught trespassing on private property to go fishing.

The plane takes off, but all I can pay attention to is the soft breaths leaving her lips.

I ignore the flight attendant when she comes around with drinks and snacks.

I ignore the person on the aisle seat when he tries to strike up a conversation with me.

I ignore the way my heart swells when she sighs in her sleep and snuggles deeper into me.

Chapter 4

Mia

"Mmm," Ryan moans as his arms pull me closer.

I'm not stiff in his arms, but there's a tension building in my blood that keeps me from clinging to him like I've done the other times I've woken up like this.

We've been in New Mexico at the Cerberus MC clubhouse for nearly a week, and still, I wake up every morning wondering where I am and if today is the day they track me down and drag me back to that compound in Miami.

"You're safe, Sweet Mia," he grumbles before pressing his lips to the top of my head.

Sweet Mia.

He started calling me that after we got off the plane, and I haven't told him to stop even though the smoothness of the nickname makes me want to cringe. There's nothing sweet about me. I'm tainted, polluted, and infected by the things that happened to me. I feel filthy, like waking up in his arms does nothing but soil him, too.

"Shower?" he grumbles, already accustomed to the routine.

I keep my back to him as he climbs out of bed. I know he needs a few minutes to himself in the mornings, and I've done my very best to ignore the erection he wakes up with each day. I know it's natural, something he can't control, just like Jason couldn't control it, but the first time I noticed it straining in his sleep pants, I freaked out, terrified he was going to take something I wasn't offering. Mornings were the worst times back at the compound, and the heightened fear of waking up back there combined with the sight of his arousal really messed me up.

He skirts around the bed, swinging the bathroom door closed so he can piss before he comes back out to let me know that the shower is on and ready. Keeping my eyes low, I walk around him into the bathroom, but he doesn't leave like he tried to do the first night in the hotel after I was discharged from the hospital. He follows me inside, closing us into the bathroom and locking the door, but he falters when he reaches for the bag to cover my cast.

"I was thinking," he begins, but there's an unease to his tone that I don't like.

I swallow as I raise my eyes to his, only momentarily distracted by the tattoos covering his chest, full left arm, and right forearm. I've been tempted to trace the islander-type ink on his skin more than once, but I figured touching him that way would be crossing a line and giving him permission to touch my skin, and that's not something I can handle.

"Tell me to go fuck myself if you need to, but—" He turns from me, bending low to pull a pair of scissors and electric clippers from under the sink.

Tears immediately well in my eyes, making the smile I almost had from the way he talks to me like I'm an old friend fade into a distant memory. I knew this was coming. It's something I've wanted to do since the very first time I looked at myself in the mirror at the hospital. My vanity isn't something I'm proud of. There are so many other things to worry about now, but my long, gorgeous hair isn't that anymore. It's dry and brittle from weeks of malnourishment and dehydration, and there are chunks missing, some down to my scalp in places from the men cutting it to keep pieces for trophies.

His face falls when he turns around to present me with the tools. My fingers grow sore from twisting them together in front of me, but I give him a nod.

"I can have one of the other girls come in and do this. They may be able to do a better job."

He must be talking about Emmalyn, the club president's wife, or even Misty, the nice lady who stops by to visit periodically. They each give me the space I need, hovering in the doorway to speak, but I don't want anyone here to witness this. Hell, I don't even want Ryan to participate, but I know I won't be able to do it with one arm.

"It's fine," I mumble, hating the huskiness of my own voice, knowing it won't get any better unless I start talking more often.

Tears stain the front of Ryan's borrowed shirt as he first uses the scissors to clip away the remaining long strands. My shoulders cool when the hair falls to the bathroom floor, but it's the sound of the buzzing clippers that make me sob the hardest.

Knowing it needs to be done, Ryan doesn't falter once he gets started. He doesn't speak over the hum like he normally would when he knows I'm anxious, and for once, I'm grateful for the reprieve. I love hearing his stories, but a distraction is the last thing I want right now. As each piece falls to my lap and surrounds my feet, I can't help but wonder if my hair was what drew that man in the parking lot to me, and with each strand that's cut away I feel freer, safer from the possibility of it ever happening again.

"It'll grow back," Ryan assures me when he turns the clippers off and sets them aside.

When I stand, I reach for the clumps lying on the floor, but his hand on my shoulder halts me.

"Don't worry about the mess. I'll clean it up. Here." When I look up, he's holding the plastic bag for my arm.

The steam from the shower fills the room, casting us in a damp halo that makes things seem a little easier than they actually are.

Remaining speechless as he secures the bag isn't new. It's like this every day, and just like every other morning, I don't step back to get undressed until after he brushes his lips across my forehead.

"Jump in the shower," he says with a smile. "You stink."

This morning his teasing doesn't put a smile on my face. This morning I'm too burdened, too stuck in my own head to appreciate his efforts.

His lips turn down in a frown before he can stop himself, but he doesn't say anything as he turns around to face the closed door, giving me the privacy I need to get undressed and into the shower.

I don't bother to hide my tears or muffle the sobs that rack my body as I use more shampoo than necessary to wash my now bald head. The shower is one place I can grieve where Ryan doesn't run to me to ease my pain. The tears are usually cathartic, mixing with the warm water before disappearing down the drain, but this morning they only seem to bring more pain.

I'm sick and tired of crying, of being afraid of my own shadow. I'm disgusted with myself for holding onto this stranger, and he has to be feeling the same way. Although he hasn't said a negative word, I know he has to be getting tired of my neediness and the pity party I can't seem to drag myself out of.

The psychiatrist who visited my hospital room before I left told me that things like this take time, that getting over the atrocious things that happened to me wouldn't happen overnight. He expected things to get worse before they got better. He recommended a daily routine, but also trying new things, finding happiness in situations I could control before branching out and being more adventurous.

I could laugh at the memory if I weren't so beat down right now.

Adventurous?

The most adventure I'd seen since arriving here was following Ryan out of this room in the middle of the night to grab something to eat, but one of the other guys was also burning the midnight oil, and I hightailed it back to the room before we even made it out of the hallway.

"Mia?" Ryan says. "Did you hear me?"

"What?" I croak.

Is he putting his foot down, telling me I have to get my shit together and get back to my own room?

They offered me one, and I stood in the middle of it for all of twenty seconds before I followed Ryan to his room and crawled in his bed without even asking permission. Max frowned before trying to tell me it wasn't healthy, but Ryan told him to shut the hell up and ushered him out of his room.

"I think you'd enjoy the New Year's party happening later."

My body freezes, hand turning to cement on my thigh as I wash. Parties at the compound were always happening, but Thanksgiving was brutal, the holiday serving as a vacation for many men who arrived looking for a good time. Many women participated, seemingly willingly to avoid the punishment that came with saying no, but I never was able to manage it. I fought every single time, and unfortunately, it's exactly what a number of them enjoyed the most. I swallow, shoving down those thoughts before they can manifest into something worse than the tremble in my hands and racing heart.

"It's just going to be the guys. Em and Misty will be there. You can meet Makayla and Khloe. I think socializing will be good for you."

Anger seeps in, and I'm glad it's replacing the terror that's threatening. Anger is something I can handle.

Who the hell does he think he is? This man doesn't know a damn thing about me other than I was an idiot and fell for a pretty-boy smile in a parking lot that landed me straight into the pits of hell for seven weeks. Shit, he doesn't even know that much. I haven't confessed a word about the day I was taken.

With rough, pissed off hands, I climb out of the shower and towel my skin dry as best I can. The absence of my hair makes things a ton easier and that makes me even more bitter. I hate everything that was taken from me. I hate being here. I hate needing him to comfort me, and most of all, I hate being weak and fragile, terrified of my own damn shadow.

The Mia Vazquez that existed a year ago wouldn't take shit from anyone. That girl would've been dead inside of a couple of days inside the compound. She would've willingly died before letting those men take from her. That girl was gone long before that guy grinned at me with what I thought was charisma and charm that transformed into hate and malicious intent by the time he tied me up and shoved that bag over my head.

Jason made sure that I was already beaten down and mostly broken by the time I was abducted. Jason put himself first, making sure to remind me that his job was more important than mine. It paid the bills my hourly wage at the specialty print shop couldn't even begin to touch. It didn't matter that my last year of college was spent crying for my dead brother until I got the notice that I flunked out. It didn't matter that I was so overcome with grief that I didn't even care about my own life until it was too late to go back and finish school so I could be a rock star in public relations like I'd always dreamed. My dreams didn't matter then, and they sure as hell don't matter now.

I shove my legs through a pair of cotton panties that I wouldn't have been caught dead in months ago before tugging on a pair of sweatpants and a t-shirt. Both belong to Ryan, both too big for me, and I can't even be bothered to care.

I shove past him, swinging the door open so fast the doorknob would probably dent the plaster if he didn't catch it before it hit.

"Mia?" Concern laces his tone, but I ignore him as I climb right back in his bed.

I'm pissed, but I'm not foolish enough to think I can make it down the hall to the room they offered me unscathed. People are always milling about, keeping their distance, or offering me food or an opportunity to join them in some frivolous activity.

"What's going on?" Ryan asks as he climbs in behind me on the bed.

I rip the covers up to my shoulder, burying my face in them and both loving and hating that they smell like his skin. I'm surrounded by him constantly, and most days, it's a relief knowing he's right there beside me. But today it just grates on my nerves.

I stiffen when he clasps my shoulder, trying to pull me so I'll either turn over to face him or snuggle against him.

"Don't," I hiss, and he releases me immediately.

"It was only a suggestion," he offers. "We can stay right here tonight if that's what you want. I'll make us a plate from the kitchen, and we can continue our movie marathon."

I don't turn and yell at him. I don't open my mouth to explain why I hate everything about what he's just offered. I don't tell him to leave, that he needs to get a life rather than being perfectly fine holing himself away.

I don't do any of that, but when he sighs and rolls to his back as he begins telling me about going stag to his senior prom because the girl he wanted to go with had the flu, I let my eyes flutter closed and I fall asleep to the only comforting voice I'm beginning to hate for no other reason than knowing I don't deserve his kindness.

Chapter 5

Scooter

Shitty moods and silent attitude aren't new for Mia. The only difference is that today, I'm somehow the focus of her irritation when normally it's focused on Max or the pillows that don't feel just right. She prefers my chest to anything else, but she didn't want me near her at all this morning.

I let her sleep, which she does more than anything, but after watching the TV on mute for eight hours, only leaving the bed to make us lunch before she rolled over and went right back to sleep, I couldn't take it any longer.

I used to find solitude in my room, needing the peace and comfort that those four walls awarded me after a long day's work, but today it was just too much.

I left Max with her, instructing him to come get me if there was an issue. The fucker better because he'll have an ass whipping coming if I go back to my room and find her upset. Suggesting the party was a mistake. I see that now, but she's going to have to leave that room, eventually.

"How's she doing?" Rocker asks, interrupting the insistency filling my legs to go check on her.

"She's the same," I mutter before titling my beer back up to my lips.

I've given myself a two-drink maximum tonight, refusing to get sloppy drunk like I normally would on New Year's Eve. I should be drinking vodka so she can't smell it on my breath. I shouldn't do anything that may trigger a bad memory for her, but I don't think I'd be able to stop myself if I started with the heavy stuff.

"Did you try to convince her to join us?" Rocker angles his head toward the younger crowd, the kids of the original Cerberus crew. "They seem like a lively bunch having fun."

"She wasn't interested." That's the watered-down truth, but I don't feel like discussing Mia with anyone.

"Oh, shit," Jinx chuckles as he slides up to us. "Did you see who just walked in? I got a hundred on Dominic."

I look over at the front door, watching as Tug walks in with Dominic's daughter on his arm. She's gorgeous in her own right. Hell, even though they're way too young for me, I can see the beauty in all of the women. Jasmine is the oldest of the group, having been adopted by

Dominic when she was young, going by the gossip floating around the clubhouse.

Jealousy seeps into my bones when I look at the group Rocker indicated earlier. So many of them are paired off and completely in love. Even at twenty and twenty-one, those kids have found their soulmates.

I shake the thought away, taking another long pull on my beer before turning my back on the group. It doesn't take long before Tug walks toward us. I knew he'd seek me out first thing. He was friends with Max and Mia going way back, and I know he's worried about her. He checked up on her a few times by text while she was still in the hospital, but it's been radio silence since we returned. I figure Max has been keeping him up to date.

Predicting where Tug is heading, Dominic makes his way to our group first, and like the sneaky assholes that they are, Rocker and Jinx slink away toward the pool tables. I'm not usually uncomfortable around any of the original members, even though they're technically my bosses, but the last time we gathered like this was Snatch's daughter's wedding, and Tug literally got caught with his pants down. In addition, Max was there participating as well. I don't know the finite details, but the gist isn't pretty.

My palms begin to sweat as Tug joins us. Dominic hasn't said a word as he lingers, but he shakes Tug's hand when he's within reach.

"Glad to see you guys here tonight," Dominic tells my teammate.

Tug nods. "We wouldn't miss it."

They chatter back and forth for a few more minutes, and I don't think I've ever witnessed a more awkward conversation before in my life.

Dominic excuses himself and walks away, and when I turn back to Tug, he releases a whoosh of air from his mouth.

"That was intense," I say with a chuckle that doesn't even begin to ease the tension surrounding the man.

"How's Mia?" Tug asks rather than bitching about his girlfriend's dad.

"About the same," I tell him just like I did Rocker a few minutes ago.

"I never thought she'd let you walk away from her," he says absently as his eyes focus across the room on Jasmine.

"She didn't."

Tug frowns, turning his attention back to me.

"What's that supposed to mean?" he snaps.

"She's here," I tell him softly, unsure of why I'm whispering. Everyone here, except him clearly, knows that Mia came back with me from Florida

"She's here?" His head jerks around, scanning the room as if he's certain she's going to pop out and surprise him.

"She's in my room," I explain.

"No, shit? I can't imagine that went over well with her parents or Max."

"It didn't," I huff. "I can barely get the man out of my room long enough to get some sleep myself."

It's the truth. Max hovers more than a dog waiting to be fed.

"What? Max is here?"

I nod, wondering if he started drinking before they showed up. This shouldn't be news. From what I gathered, Max, Jasmine, and Tug have had some sort of relationship going on for a while now. Surely his sister being in New Mexico would be something he brought up to his lovers.

"How long has he been here?"

Then again, maybe not.

"We came back the day after Christmas."

"A week?" he hisses.

He doesn't give me time to answer before he's storming off in the direction of my room. He's too fast, and I'm not able to grab him before he wrenches my door open.

"Are you fucking kidding me?" Tug snaps as soon as the door swings open. "You're here?"

"Don't wake her," I hear Max say from my spot in the hallway. "We can talk in the hall."

"I think we're going to need a little more privacy than that," Tug snaps before grabbing the front of Max's t-shirt and shoving him into another room.

I ignore whatever is going on with those two grown-ass men and close myself into my room. After brushing my teeth, I change into my pajamas and join Mia on the bed. Unlike earlier when she didn't want to have a damn thing to do with me, she turns in her sleep and rests her head again my chest. Finally, everything is right in my world.

***

A knock on the door startles me awake, and if it weren't for the sun trying to infiltrate the room through the curtains, I'd kill the motherfucker standing on the other side.

I know who it is before I climb out of bed, so I take a few minutes to get myself under control. I'm frustrated every morning when I wake up with a cock ready to take on the world. And even though Mia had a rough night last night, burdened with nightmares that made her whimper and cry out in her sleep, my dick still won't behave.

She whimpers when I slip out from under her, but quiets when I press my lips to her temple and promise her I'll be right back. Before standing, I squeeze the tip of my dick until the pain causes it to get the message.

Don't get me wrong, I'm not all sexed up and ready to fuck a broken girl who is years away from any sort of intimacy, but my cock doesn't understand a gorgeous woman sleeping on top of us all night without getting a little action. He's bitter, and I'm embarrassed.

I could blame nature, but the erections I get around her are all one hundred percent due to her and have minimal impact from natural causes.

"What?" I hiss the second I pull open the door.

"How is she doing?"

"She's fucking sleeping, Max."

Even though I don't think the fucker deserves it, I push open the door wide enough so that he can see her resting form on the bed. Her forehead furrows when the light hits her face, so I close it a little.

"I want to see her," he insists.

"I said she's sleeping," I repeat, anger growing exponentially every second I have to stand here and repeat myself to a grown man.

With more anger than I've seen Max display, he clenches his fists and puffs his chest out like he's going to punch me in the face. I raise an eyebrow at him in challenge, wondering if kicking his ass would be just what I need to let off the steam that's been building since I saw Mia's reaction to him being alive in the hospital.

What sick fuck, regardless of what he had going on, lets his family believe he's dead for ten years?

"I want to see her," he seethes, spittle forming on his lower lip.

"Nothing has changed in the last seven hours, Max. Let her rest," I say with more patience than I feel right now.

Mia wouldn't be impressed if I kicked his ass, and the sound of her low whimper behind me is the only thing that saves me from rearranging this dick's face.

"Why is she upset?" Max questions.

"Because she's fitful when I leave," I answer. "Let me get back to her."

"This isn't healthy," Max whispers with resignation in his voice. I watch him as the anger drains from his body. He slumps forward; shoulders bent, leaving him looking defeated and broken. "She needs to face what's happened, so she can begin to heal."

"And she'll do that when she's ready," I remind him, not for the first time. The man is driving me crazy, but I also need to take a step back and try to picture how I'd respond if it were my sister. It's difficult to do since I'm an only child, but I have cousins I'd go to the ends of the earth for, so I sort of get where he's coming from.

"She won't ever be ready if you continue to coddle her. You're only letting her get lost in her head."

Mia's whimpers grow louder, and without a word, I step back and close the door in Max's face.

"Shhh, Sweet Mia," I whisper as I climb right back into bed with her.

She doesn't waste a second before wrapping her arm around my stomach and resting her head right back on my chest like I never left to begin with.

Max's words filter through my mind as I run my hand up and down Mia's back, but even though I know he's speaking the truth, I can't help but feel like I'm exactly where I'm meant to be.

Chapter 6

Mia

Pretending to be asleep is easier, so when Ryan climbs back in bed, I settle on his chest with every intention of sleeping the entire day away.

The comfort he provides is my happy place. It's where I can imagine a different life, one without trauma and pain. It doesn't last long. Ryan is too perceptive, and I'm not a very good faker when it comes to sleep. I blame it on my body being in a constant state of apprehension while I'm awake, and he easily picks up on that fact.

"Ready to get the day started?"

Instead of verbally responding, I nuzzle his chest. He chuckles, the vibrations bouncing against my cheek, and I can't help the smile that tugs up the corners of my lips. I itch to press my lips to his t-shirt, but I don't. He already holds me every night, I don't want to pressure him into being more.

As we lie there silently, I think about what my life has become, starting back to a couple years ago when things turned sour with Jason. I was in a rut long before I was abducted, and like a light bulb going off in my dark existence, I realize I'm the only one that can change things. I'm the only one who can rise out of this bed and be different today from who I was yesterday. Max talks a big game about Ryan not coddling me, but at the end of the day I know my brother wouldn't force me to act the way he expects either.

With renewed determination, I sit up on the side of the bed, refusing to look back at Ryan for reassurance. He's a crutch I've leaned on too much the last week and since today is a new year, I decide I also need to be a new me. Cheesy, I know, but changes need to be made, nonetheless.

"Shower?" Ryan asks as I head to the bathroom.

I nod before closing myself inside to take care of normal bathroom business. He opens the door when he hears the water in the sink as I begin to brush my teeth. When I'm done, he wraps my arm in the plastic bag, and I'm counting down the days until I can be self-sufficient enough to manage a damn shower on my own.

Once the bag is secure, I stand by the door with an eyebrow raised. Instead of the irritation I expect, Ryan winks at me and leaves the bathroom.

"I'll be right out here if you need me," he says before I can close myself in the bathroom alone.

I still tremble as I wash. Tears still leak from my eyes when I once again pour too much shampoo in my hand for my bald head, and I expect it'll be awhile before I get used to using the correct amount. It may take longer than it should since I avoid looking in the mirror. I can't stand to see the yellowing bruises all over my body. It's bad enough that I still ache in dozens of places where I was hit and kicked hard enough that my muscles ache.

Toweling dry is easier today than it ever has been because I don't have to keep my eyes locked on Ryan's back wondering if today is going to be the day he turns around, disregarding my privacy before he takes from me what he thinks he's owed for the help and comfort he's provided.

Deep in my gut, I know he isn't that type of man. He's proved it over and over, so many times I lost count, but it doesn't stop my traumatized brain from creating scenarios where he turns into the villain and hurts me.

More tears spring from my eyes at the realization that I'll probably never be able to trust another living person again. That level of awareness brings a wash of sadness, but I straighten my spine as I struggle into fresh clothes. Only moments ago I resolved myself to doing better today than I did yesterday, and it's too soon to already start back peddling now.

"All done?" Ryan asks from the bed.

He's lounged back on a pile of pillows with the TV remote sitting in his lap. He's the epitome of cool and casual, but the way he chews on the inside of his cheek as his eyes scan my body betrays his easy demeanor. He's not the only one good at reading people.

"I'm good," I tell him, knowing that the first part of my getting-better plan needs to include more talking.

I've avoided all forms of conversation, afraid that speaking will lead to questions because people will think that I'm ready to talk about what happened. What they don't know is that day will never come. I want to burn those memories from my brain, not talk out loud about them.

"I'm next," he says as he pops off the bed and slides past me to head into the bathroom for his own shower. "Give me five minutes, and then I'll go get us breakfast."

We literally switch places; him in the shower and me against the pillows as I flip through dozens of channels, finding absolutely nothing to watch.

The water shuts off, but before he has enough time to dress, the bathroom door cracks open releasing a puff of steam around Ryan.

His head pokes out, and I'm struck speechless. I can't focus on his face because the sight of his bare shoulder hypnotizes me. He's rock-solid, and even though he's worked out in the room while I watched, he's always had a shirt on. He's always been clothed, but right now as my eyes trail down his side, it's clear he's only wrapped in a fluffy towel.

My fingers begin to tremble when he shifts his weight, my eyes darting to the bedroom door that leads into the hallway, and that sadness I felt in the bathroom earlier returns since my first instinct is to get away from him. He's too close to naked, too close to revealing the parts of a man's body that's designed to take a woman.

"Mia?"

Tears bead on my lashes as my eyes meet his.

"What's wrong?" He swings the door open, gripping his towel at the waist and walks a few steps deeper in the room.

"Please don't," I beg, cringing further away with every inch he draws closer.

"Fuck," he spits. "I'm not going to hurt you. I forgot my clothes."

Without another word, he turns toward the closet, closing the door behind him, and it seems like an eternity before the door opens again to reveal him fully dressed with a cautious look on his face.

"It won't happen again," he tells me, standing on the other side of the room and giving me enough space to get things right in my head again. "Our routine was thrown off this morning. I just forgot my clothes."

"It's fine," I mumble.

"It's not. I know your brain won't let you trust, and I get that, but please know I'd never hurt you."

"I know," I tell him, and in someplace, deep in my heart, I do know that, or at least I want to believe that, but today isn't that day, unfortunately.

"Did you want me to go make breakfast?" He gives me a weak smile, knowing that morning time is when I'm the hungriest. My appetite wanes as the day goes by, and I'm certain it has everything to do with the stress building up over the daylight hours.

"Yes," I tell him. "Can I go with you?"

I give him my best practiced smile, hoping he buys it, when really the four walls of the bedroom feel like they're closing in on me for the first time. Normally, I find sanctuary in here, but today it's just too much.

"Really?" A genuine grins spreads across his face. "I'd love that."

My hand trembles in his as we step out into the hallway, but as always, he's patient with me, letting me stop and listen to the sounds of the building before taking another step down the hall.

"It's going to be pretty quiet today. Most of the guys will be sleeping off hangovers from the party last night," Ryan explains as we inch our way toward the kitchen.

I freeze on the threshold of the kitchen, but the man in the corner doesn't even look up from his coffee cup as we enter. Ryan uses a bent knuckle to nudge my head up.

"Eggs and bacon?" he asks as if the two of us standing in the kitchen is an everyday occurrence instead of it being my first time to venture out this far since I got here over a week ago.

"Eggs and toast?" I counter.

If he's disappointed, his face doesn't show it. Bacon takes too long to cook, and I don't know how long I'm going to be able to stand being in here.

"Why don't you make our coffee." He points to the station that's thankfully on the opposite side of the room from where the guy is sitting. "That's Jinx. He won't bother you. The man doesn't even speak until his third cup of coffee. I like mine black with a little sugar."

With a gentle hand at the small of my back, Ryan urges in the direction of the already brewed coffee. The station is set off to itself, but it's on an island, as if these guys need space around the entire thing to line up and serve themselves. I'm grateful because it allows me to stand on the far side and keep an eye on the entire room as I make our cups.

As I'm reaching for the sugar, another man walks in. He's shirtless with pajama pants that are only staying up by the juts of his hips. He doesn't seem to notice me as he rubs his eyes, but his destination is clear.

The sugar jar, glass with a metal lid like the ones you'd find at a hotel or diner, falls from my hand, clanking on the granite countertop of the coffee station.

The guy walking toward me looks up, freezing like he's been struck, but thankfully the noise also draws Ryan's attention.

"Rocker," Ryan snaps, "go get dressed."

Scooter: Cerberus MC Book 11 | 40

"Sorry," the man mutters, looking sincerely apologetic for startling me. "Good morning, Mia."

He turns around and leaves without another word.

"Don't forget a little sugar in mine," Ryan says as he situates himself in front of the huge stove.

He doesn't make a big deal out of my negative reaction to his friend. He acts as if nothing happened at all.

I nod, picking the sugar jar back up and sprinkling a little into his coffee before using a wooden stir stick to mix it well. My raging pulse and the spike of adrenaline makes me rush to his side, but I somehow manage doing so without spilling any of the coffee on my hands or the floor.

"Scrambled okay?"

I nod even though it's not my favorite way to eat eggs because it's the fastest way to get them on the plate and eaten so we can get out of here and back to the room that only moments ago was driving me crazy.

Ryan makes small talk as he cooks, instructing me to the toaster, and not frowning or looking disappointed when I end up right by his side.

When he's done, and without me asking, he situates us on the far side of the room, tucked away but with the ability to see the entire room.

I scarf down my eggs and toast, wanting to rush through breakfast, but Ryan eats slowly, each bite deliberately chewed as if he's concerned about his digestive health. I want to tilt his head back, wedge open his mouth and pour his breakfast down his throat because he's taking so long, but I end up distracted by a young girl that walks in. Dressed in nothing but a thigh-length silk robe, she's disheveled and looks exhausted, and she doesn't seem happy to be here. I don't know much about biker gangs, and Ryan has assured me more than once that they're not anything like what I would've seen on TV or watched in some criminal documentary, but the evidence of this place being like those shows is walking like a zombie to the coffee pot.

Makeup is smudged on her face, and her hair is worse than a rat's nest. She looks used and uncaring of her appearance, and her eyes are empty, much like many of the girls back at the compound.

I don't realize I'm trembling until Ryan lays his hand over the top of mine.

"Hey, Gigi," Ryan says to the woman rather than speaking to me.

She turns her head in our direction, lifting her hand for a little wave.

"Too much fun at the party last night?"

The woman, Gigi as Ryan called her, scoffs. "I wish."

She reaches for two cups before filling each to the brim.

"Amelia is teething again. We were both up all night trying to soothe her. See ya later."

She shuffles out of the kitchen, a cup of coffee in each hand.

"That's Kincaid's daughter. Well, one of them. She has a twin. She's also with Hound, and they have a baby together."

"She doesn't seem happy to be here," I mutter, even though I saw the missing spark in her eyes reignite when she spoke about her daughter.

"I imagine mornings are rough after tending to a cranky baby all night," he says. "She's usually more put together than that."

"The president lets his underage daughter stay in a relationship with one of his bikers."

He smiles at me, his eyes darting back and forth between mine.

"What?" My eyebrows draw together.

"I never thought that we'd be talking about someone else when you finally decided that talking can be a good thing."

I roll my eyes, focusing on my empty coffee cup on the table rather than responding to him.

"Gigi is twenty-one, maybe twenty-two. I can't really keep track. She's grown, and I don't know much about her, but I do know that I don't think Kincaid could've stopped what was going on between those two. If you ever see them together, you'll understand."

"I'm sor—"

Ryan's phone rings in his pocket before I can finish apologizing for jumping to the wrong conclusion. Instead of silencing it like he normally does, he stands from the table.

"I have to take. I'll be right back."

Thankfully he doesn't go far. I can still see his shoulder on the other side of the kitchen door. Jinx left before we plated our breakfast, so I'm the only one in here right now. After being snapped at by Ryan, Rocker didn't even come back to make a cup of coffee.

"I can't," Ryan hisses into the phone. "I told you why."

My head tilts as I try to listen harder.

"Seriously, Kirsty. Now isn't a good time." He sighs again. "I don't know. I'm helping her. She needs me. We've discus—"

He growls, pulling the phone away from his ear, making it clear that the woman on the other end isn't happy and hung up on him.

I snap my eyes back down to my plate before he turns to come back in.

Sorrow clogs my throat with the realization that I've kept this man from his life for the better part of two weeks. I didn't ask if he had a girlfriend or a significant other in his life, yet here I am coming in between what he has with her.

This is unacceptable, and since it's a new year, things will change today.

Chapter 7

Scooter

"You okay?" I lean in close to Mia so she's the only one that can hear my question.

She nods but refuses to meet my eyes.

I thought her going to the kitchen was a huge step. I tried my damnedest to make her comfortable, keeping the conversation going and not making a big deal when she clearly freaked first with Jinx sitting at the table and again when Rocker walked in without a shirt on, but it may have been too much for her.

Now we're sitting in the living room as it fills up with bedraggled Cerberus men, and she's frozen beside me. I've asked more than once if she wanted to head back to my room, but each time she's shaken her head no, refusing to leave her spot on the sofa beside me.

Her eyes dart everywhere, taking in the men playing pool, the two talking near the stereo system, and the couple of guys bantering playfully near the foosball table.

Every once in a while, a shiver runs up her spine, but she's made no move to get up and leave.

As the minutes pass, my concern for her only grows. I'm relieved she's wanting to hang out and leave the confines of the bedroom, but it seems like it's more to her detriment than helping her ease back into things.

Things were looking up. She spoke more at the breakfast table than she ever has in one sitting when Gigi walked out, but now her lips are clamped shut. I have no idea where Max is, but I find myself wishing he was here with us, if only to add another person around her that makes her more comfortable.

A yell from the other side of the room draws my attention, but it's more of a casual look in the direction of the guys as they bump chests, arguing mildly over a lost game of pool.

It's more for Mia I realize when she begins to shake uncontrollably.

"Act like men or go to your rooms," Hound mutters as he walks past Jinx and Grinch.

"He fucking cheated," Grinch sneers.

"Winning isn't cheating, asshole," Jinx counters. "Quit being a fucking baby."

They shove each other, but it's not like they're going to go to full-out blows, but when I turn to face Mia to assure her that everything is fine, her hands are clamped on the hem of her shirt so tight her knuckles are turning white.

"Ready to go?" I ask again.

Her head works up and down at a violent rate, but it seems she's unable to take her eyes off the guys arguing across the room. I have no idea why she's reacting this way, but maybe she saw some pretty violent shit back in Miami.

I don't question her in front of everyone. I simply pick her up and walk out of the room with her. As if she's come to her senses, she wiggles to get out of my arms when we make it to the entrance to the hallway.

"They won't hurt each other. We're all like brothers, and even though I don't really know what that was like growing up, I can tell you that men argue and fight, and then things are back to normal."

Raucous laughter filters in at our backs proving my point. The timing is perfect, but Mia is already too rattled. I urge her down the hall to my room, but she stops a door short and pushes open the door to the room she was offered when we first arrived. I don't think she's been in here since that first day, but I watch, bewildered as she steps inside. She closes the door in my face before I can ask her what's going on.

I raise my knuckles to knock, but let my arm drop before I manage it. If she needs space, I have to give it to her. I can't force myself on her. That would be too reminiscent of the things I'm sure she went through before, and I refuse to even make her think for a second that I'm anything like those pieces of shit.

Even though I don't knock, her being locked away doesn't keep me from pacing the hallway for the next twenty minutes, waiting for her to step back out to look for me. When it doesn't happen, I go to my room, leaving the door wide open, and wait for her there.

She never comes. The door to that room doesn't open, and when I convince myself that she's probably fallen asleep, I leave my room. I'm not a weirdo. I only press my ear to the door for a few seconds, and I walk away when I'm met with nothing but silence.

Most of the guys are still in the living room, but since I don't feel like socializing, I walk out the front door and head to the garage. Jinx and Grinch gave up on the game of pool, and they're currently huddled around the space heater near Shadow's project bike.

"Didn't mean to scare your girl," Jinx mutters.

"If you didn't cheat, we could've avoided the entire situation," Grinch argues.

"You guys are like three-year-olds," I mutter as I join them.

I didn't think to grab a jacket, and even though the garage keeps the wind out, it's fucking cold right now. I breathe into my hands, rubbing them together in front of my face to warm them faster. I really wanted some peace and fucking quiet, but I knew it was a long shot. There are ten Cerberus men, not including the original guys, and short of holing up in my room, I know I'm bound to run into one or three of these fuckers.

"Everyone else comes back tomorrow," Grinch says. "Means we're that much closer to going and setting Venezuela on fire."

We all grin. I've been focused on Mia, but I haven't forgotten for one second what we'll be facing soon. My blood burns with the need for some vengeance, and even though I know that's just about as dangerous as heading into a mission with personal shit hovering over me, it won't stop me from taking my pound of flesh.

If there was a way for me to drag Luiz Jiménez back to New Mexico so Mia could be the one to put a bullet between his eyes, I'd make it happen and call it a late Christmas gift. Even if that were a possibility; however, I know that it wouldn't change much for her. Killing the man responsible would only be a Band-Aid over the wounds that were inflicted on her.

"I heard talk that Kincaid is bringing in additional men," Jinx says, keeping the conversation going.

"That would help," Grinch mutters. "But hired men can be more of a hindrance."

"Naw." Jinx shakes his head. "We had to do it three years ago in South Africa. The guys he hires are top notch. Patriots through and through."

Grinch and I both nod, happy with the news. There's nothing worse than facing a life or death situation and not knowing if you can trust the guy at your six.

"It's fucking cold out here," Jinx hisses when it's clear the heater is fighting a losing battle with the cold.

"Yeah," I agree, feeling like I've already left Mia alone for too long.

She may not want to be around me, but my skin is itchy, needing to feel her against me.

"I'm going back in. See ya." I walk away from the guys who continue to grumble about the cold but make no move to head inside where it's warmer.

Kincaid stops me in the living room before I can get back to Mia.

"How's she doing?" he asks. "Some of the guys said she finally came out of the room for a while."

"She's taking it one day at a time." I run my hands over my cold head, still regretting that I didn't wear a jacket or a beanie outside. It's going to take me forever to warm back up.

I know the quickest way to make that happen, but my president is standing between me and my little living furnace right now.

"I can have Emmalyn and Misty spend some time with her if you think that will help. They're both chomping at the bit to get to know her better."

"They've stopped by the room a couple of times, and Mia knows the offer is always on the table. She'll accept when she's ready."

Kincaid nods, giving me that same sad look Max did this morning when he woke us up.

"Just let me know," he says with a quick nod before walking away.

The door to her room is still closed, and mine is open and empty, but I've given her space, given her time to come to terms with being outside of the room a little, and now I have to see her. I have to know that she's alright and offer the strength of my arms if she needs them. Not once since she reached for me in the hospital have I needed distance from her. If anything, I've grown addicted to the way her body curves around mine, each and every one of her curves fitting perfectly into mine. Enough is enough.

I knock softly on her door, increasing the force when she doesn't answer. By the time I'm ready to pound on the damn thing, I announce myself and turn the knob. She isn't on the bed, and after further inspection of the bathroom and closet, I realize she isn't in here at all.

I check my room again, sprinting to open my bathroom and closet doors. My heart is pounding in my chest making that and my rough breaths the only thing I can hear.

I rush to the kitchen. She isn't there either. She's not in the living room, and the people hanging out haven't seen her.

"Maybe she went to the pool?" Rocker offers.

"It's fucking twenty-five degrees outside," I hiss. "She's not fucking swimming."

It doesn't stop me from checking there though and by the time I make it back inside everyone is huddled in a group, as if they already know that I'm about to ask them to help me find her.

Before I can give them instructions, I pull my phone from my pocket, hating that I'm fixing to have to give her brother this news. The phone rings and goes to voicemail over and over, but just when I'm fixing to press the call button for the sixth time, the phone rings in my hand, and Max shows up on the screen.

"What's wrong?" Max asks instead of giving some contrived greeting.

"It's Mia," I tell him, sucking air into my lungs, but still unable to get enough oxygen to my brain. "She's gone. We can't find her anywhere."

He tells me he's on his way before he hangs up.

"Tell us what to do," Jinx says.

I'm unable to speak. I was responsible for this girl and now she's gone. This failure is on me.

Kincaid steps forward, places a hand on my shoulder, and addresses the crowd, "Listen up. This is what we need to do."

Chapter 8

Mia

Cold doesn't even begin to describe the state I'm in right now.

Chilled to the bone and near hypothermia is a much better description, but even though I can no longer feel my feet in the borrowed mud boots I found on the back porch of the clubhouse, I keep on walking.

My mind doesn't clear with the distance I create between myself and the clubhouse. My body doesn't grow more relaxed the further I get from Ryan. I'm only filled with dread and a constant feeling that's been telling me I'm an idiot and making a huge mistake since I took the first step off the property.

It has to be below freezing, and after being in Miami and before that balmy Louisiana, my body is in no way able to deal with the frigid wind beating against my face as I stay off the road, hovering near the tree line.

I don't know north from south or east from west, and even if I had a clue which direction the nearest town was in, I'm so directionally challenged that I'd probably still miss it.

I didn't really think this through. All I know is continuing to be a burden to Ryan and every other member of the Cerberus MC ends today. I've taken over their lives. Even Rocker couldn't stumble to the coffee pot shirtless without me freaking out and Ryan insisting that he leave. If their bitterness about me being there hasn't started yet, it will soon.

Ryan with his phone call to his girlfriend was the final straw. I'm not his responsibility, and yet I've clasped on to the man and turned his life upside down.

No more.

No more neediness.

No more being afraid of my own shadow.

No more upending people's lives because I can't get my shit together.

Just, no more.

I should've gone back home to Louisiana with my parents. Ma wouldn't bat an eye if I didn't want to leave the house. Hell, she never wanted us to grow up and leave in the first place.

The rumble of an engine coming from the direction I began walking what seems like years ago fills my ears, and I duck further into the trees, crouching low to the ground because the leafless timber doesn't provide much cover. Thankfully, the dark clothing I'm wearing helps me to blend in with my surroundings. An SUV rolls past slowly, but I drop my head down before they pass, making it impossible for me to tell who's inside.

I plan to watch their taillights until they're a safe distance away and I can start walking again, but before they get a couple feet past my location, the brake lights flash.

I keep in my hunched-over position, whispering prayers that they'll keep going, but just like the day I was taken from the mall, my luck runs out. A man climbs out of the passenger seat, the interior light making it easy for me to see the outline of his form. At least he was smart enough to dress for the weather. The hood of his thick jacket is pulled up over his head, and it obscures his face, making it impossible to see who he is.

He looks down at some small machine in his hands, but then his eyes snap up in my direction like he can see in the dark.

The tremble that's been racking my body from the cold turns into something more. Fear like I've never felt before washes over me.

Fear is a healthy emotional response. It activates the fight-or-flight part of your brain, but when you've already faced horrific things, it's enough to make you shut down completely. Fear of the unknown is one thing. With the experiences I've already had, knowing what could happen if I'm taken again is enough for me to pray for a quick death. I'd rather curl up and die right here on some desolate road in New Mexico than end up in another compound as a plaything for sick, sadistic men.

"Mia?"

Ryan's voice startles me, and I want to run to him, but the illusion of him isn't real. He would be the first person grateful that I left, no doubt having been counting down the days until I get my shit together and disappear. I'm only wishing the man standing at the side of the SUV is once again my tattoo-covered white knight.

Before I have the wherewithal to turn and run deeper into the trees, he turns, placing the machine down on the seat, before turning and walking in my direction.

I'm frozen solid, seemingly in the real sense of the word due to the weather as well as the proverbial.

"Sweet Mia," he says as he crouches in front of me, staying on my level but not reaching for me. "What are you doing out here? You'll end up with pneumonia and frostbite."

I shake and shudder, my teeth clacking together, and no matter how hard I try to make it stop, my efforts only make things worse.

"I'm picking you up," he warns as he reaches for me, and for a moment when the moon shines on his face revealing familiar features, I let myself believe that the only man that makes things right is the one lifting me into his arms.

Here's the thing about being near death, even when parts of my body and brain are telling me to run, my heart and the bone-deep exhaustion make me believe in his sanctuary. It's foolish, and in some part of my barely functioning brain, I can appreciate that fact, but giving in and letting him carry me away is easier. Giving up is easier. And since I fought so hard back in Miami, only to become the sinister focus of so many men, I realize I'm tired of fighting.

I watched the life fade from several women's eyes. I watched them refuse to eat, which only led to the others fighting over their rejections in an effort to survive. It didn't take long for them to slip away.

That'll be my plan this go around.

But instead of rough hands, a comforting embrace engulfs my body, and instead of a whiskey and cigarette smoke stench, a familiar body wash engulfs my nose, and even with as much bravado as I left the clubhouse with, I burrow myself deeper against his chest.

Leaving was stupid, and even though I don't want to need him with the manic desperation that takes over every cell of my being, it doesn't stop it from happening.

"Sweet Mia," he coos as he carries me up the embankment toward the waiting SUV. "I've got you. We'll get you warm in no time."

"We've got her," another man says as Ryan settles in the back seat with me still against his chest.

"Get her home," an unfamiliar voice says through the Bluetooth in the vehicle. "I've already contacted Samson. Dr. Davison is on her way to assess her."

The ride back to the clubhouse is a short one, too short considering how far I thought I made it away from there. I don't bother to lift my head as Ryan carries me inside. I can sense a swarm of people watching me, but silence fills the air around us as he makes his way to his room.

All too soon he releases me, and I stand with my head hung in shame as he pulls the down comforter off his bed and wraps the thing around me until I'm cocooned in his scent and warmth. The blanket helps, but it feels like it will take days for my body to once again return to normal temperatures.

My teeth are still making noise as they smack against each other, and my hands tremble to the point that it's nearly impossible to keep my grip on the cover surrounding me. Ryan holds me to his chest, and it sinks in that I'm not going to be hurt. He's here to protect me. He's real, not some apparition disguising a malevolent person wanting to hurt me.

"You had me worried," he whispers against the top of my head.

I shake in his arms, first from the cold but then with the way his body tenses.

I blink up at him when he takes a step back and clasps me at my shoulders so he can frown down at me.

"What were you thinking? You could've fucking died out there. Leaving here was a stupid fucking cho—"

He clamps his mouth shut, the muscles in his jaw tensing over and over as he stares down at me.

He's angry, and before I can think, I lift up on my toes and press my lips to his.

Chapter 9

Scooter

Cold lips press to mine, and even though it's something I haven't let myself want, I realize immediately that it's something I've needed from her for weeks. Something that tells me she's been feeling exactly the same way about me that I have about her.

It still doesn't stop the gasp of surprise from escaping or the low moan when she presses her tongue to mine. My eyes widen in shock, but it's the sight of her eyes clenched tight as if she's in pain and the fresh tears streaming down her cheeks that make me take another step back.

My lips tingle with the loss, and my eyebrows slam together in confusion with her reaction. She kissed me. She reached up on her toes and angled her mouth to press against mine, not the other way around. So why does she look like I just forced myself on her?

"Mia?" I shake my head, trying to get a grip on the situation and also to wipe the need to kiss her again from my brain.

Her lips are still blue from being out in the cold for God knows how long, and they tremble uncontrollably. When we first came in here, she was shaking because of the cold, but now after she kissed me, I can see the fear in her eyes.

"I'm sorry," I tell her because it's the only thing I can think of right now. My mind is so clouded that just being around her makes everything so muddled.

I can't think straight when she's around. My body is in a constant state of worry, need, and concern. It's all too much for me to be able to work through in front of her. I'm terrified of coming on too strong, or not strong enough. I'm always worried I'll say the wrong thing or react to her the wrong way. It's why I've been telling her fluffy stories about my past, skipping over all the bad shit I've seen and done since becoming an adult. My one-sided conversations are nothing more than an attempt to calm her and ease her worries.

But then she goes and presses her perfect mouth to mine, and I'm struck stupid, like an idiot teenager finally getting to kiss the girl at prom.

"I shouldn't have done that," I whisper, hoping it will calm her.

But all it does is make her cry harder, the tears now rushing out of her red-rimmed eyes like I've given her horrible news.

When her shoulders slump and she stares at me with an expectation I can't decipher, I know I have to get away from her. I can't help her when my own mind and body are warring with each other. I can't comfort her when deep down I need comfort myself.

"I—" Her face contorts with more pain than I've ever seen on her face before. Even in the hospital that first day when she woke up terrified and afraid of everyone but me, I didn't see this level of agony in her dark eyes. "I can't be here right now."

I turn and leave the room, grateful that her sobs are silent because the sound of her pain would only draw me in closer to her.

"How is she?" Max asks as I step into the hallway and close my bedroom door with more restraint than I feel.

"She's cold, but she'll be fine."

"I want to see her." The man has had those five words on repeat since we got back from Miami, but tonight they agitate me more than they ever have before.

I don't need him going into that room and seeing her like she is right now. I don't need him concocting scenarios of how I may have hurt his sister, although his creative appraisal of the situation may give me some insight to what the hell is going on.

"She's going to get into a warm bath," I lie. "She wants some time alone."

He sighs, head rolling forward on his shoulders much the same way Mia's did just moments ago. "I should've been here. Why did she leave? What happened to force her out into the freezing cold?"

His barrage of questions are the very same ones I've been asking myself. Was it because of me, or is that my ego talking? Her demeanor was a little off this afternoon, which is saying a lot for a girl who has refused to leave my room for the last week, but I don't think I said or did anything to upset her.

She was scared after the guys were arguing over pool, but I figured she'd be okay once she was in a safe place.

I made a lot of assumptions, and that's the last time I'll make those mistakes again.

"I don't know why she left, but she's safe now," I grumble as Tug and Jasmine walk into the hallway.

"There you are," Tug says as he places himself right in front of Max.

Jasmine reaches for him too, and like they're all an extension of each other, Max wraps his arms around both of them and they do the same with him. It's the most sensual huddle I've ever seen, and I use the reprieve to make my escape.

Worried, questioning eyes look up at me when I walk out into the living room, but the man I need to talk to isn't in the room. Rocker and Jinx eye me expectantly, and normally I'd go to them for advice, but this goes deeper than any half-hearted conversation about women. Neither of these guys have ever been in a serious relationship, as far as I know, so they don't have the foundation I require. Not that Mia and I are in any form of relationship, but I need to figure out a way to reach that woman without scaring her to death or making things worse for her.

Unless he's home, Kincaid would be in the conference room. I turn back around and push open the heavy wooden door without knocking, finding Kincaid inside. I only consider Shadow, Snatch, Itchy, and Dominic as bonuses as I close myself inside with them.

"How is she?" Kincaid asks. "Did she bother to give an explanation?"

"She's warming up," I tell him as I fall into a chair on the side of the table. It's not the one I normally sit in but walking to the other side would take more energy than I have to give right now. "She hasn't said anything."

"Have you asked her if she wants to stay here?" Shadow asks from behind the screen of his computer.

"She wanted to be here."

"Right," Dominic says as he takes the chair across from me. "When she was in the hospital, she wanted to be here. That may have changed. The woman didn't walk out into sub-freezing temps because she loves the clubhouse. Did something happen today? Something that would've made her want to leave?"

These are all the same questions Max had, and I still don't have answers.

"She came out of the room for breakfast and hung out a little in the living room. She was upset when a couple of the guys started playfully arguing over pool," I explain. "When we left the living room, she went into the room she was offered when she first arrived. I didn't see her again until I pulled her out of the trees twenty minutes ago. No one said anything to her other than including her in conversations as best they could earlier. They didn't ask her questions or pry."

I shake my head, confusion only growing as I explain the day.

"And you were with her every single second?"

"Yes," I answer, but then shake my head. "I stepped away to take a phone call for a minute, but I was right outside of the kitchen, and she was the only one in there. She wasn't approached by anyone."

"Who called you?" Shadow asks.

I recoil, indignant and hating that my bosses are asking such personal questions, but then realization washes over me.

"Kirsty," I mutter.

"The girl you've been seeing?" Snatch clarifies.

"I wouldn't call it seeing. We aren't dating or anything, just having a little fun when time permits."

I feel like scum, and I questioning everything I've ever done in my past that may look bad in Mia's eyes.

"Think Mia may have overheard part of that conversation?" Kincaid asks.

"Possibly." I press my face into my hands. "Probably. The woman has excellent hearing."

"That explains it," Shadow adds.

"Jealousy?" I mutter. "Highly unlikely. She doesn't have shit to be jealous of."

"Because Kirsty doesn't mean anything to you or because Mia doesn't?"

I glare at Kincaid, uncaring if he's my boss in this moment or not.

"I'd lay down my life to protect Mia. She isn't just some girl to me."

"Does she know that?" Itchy asks, finally joining the conversation.

"She kissed me," I blurt.

"Before or after she heard the phone call from Kirsty?" Dominic crosses his arms over his chest, and I can't tell which way he wants my answer to go.

"After," I admit. "Like just moments ago. But when I looked at her while her lips were pressed to mine, she had her eyes squeezed shut and tears were spilling from her eyes."

"What were you doing?" Shadow asks, the topic of conversation interesting enough to finally make him pull his eyes from his computer screen.

"At first, I kissed her back, but I put an end to it when I saw how upset it was making her. I know I shouldn't have—"

Kincaid holds his hand up to silence me. "He means what were you doing right before she kissed you."

"Nothing," I answer, but I let the memory play through my head. "No, I was angry. I wasn't yelling, but I know she knew I was pissed that she put herself in danger."

"And that explains the kiss," Dominic says, leaning back in his chair.

I stare at him, more confused than ever. "That explains it? Could you please explain it to me because apparently I'm too ignorant to read between the lines?"

"We've been doing this for a long time," Kincaid begins. "We've seen the gamut of reactions of how women behave after being abducted. We've had suicides by women who just couldn't handle what happened. Hell, we had two girls go back to their captives within days of being rescued. One girl we rescued a few years ago is now living with one of the most sadistic MCs in Massachusetts."

I narrow my eyes. "Which MC?"

"The Ravens Ruin out of Sutton. Several women have gone on to join convents. My point is that we've seen a lot, but one of the most common things for one of these women to do is to protect herself. She kissed you when you were angry because she either found out that worked while she was abducted, or she saw it work for others. She was trying to calm you down. She's trying to appease her master," Kincaid finishes.

"That's fucked up," I mutter. "I'd never hurt her, and I'm not her fucking master. Owning a woman isn't something that turns me on."

"We know that. You know that, but she's still living in a different reality," Snatch says giving me a sad smile. "I imagine it started with the phone call and then seeing the guys argue made things worse. She either didn't feel safe here any longer, or she's got it in her head that she's interrupting your life."

"I don't think she feels unsafe," Dominic interjects. "I was in the SUV with him when we found her. She didn't hesitate to cling to him when he picked her up."

"Then she's feeling like a burden, and she felt like leaving was the best for everyone involved excluding herself," Shadow says. "And the kiss was her way to keep you from being mad or hating her or some other fear she's concocted in her head."

"And what do I do now?" I feel helpless, just like I do every time she cries in the shower and her nudity prevents me from going to her. It kills me when I can't comfort her and make things better.

"Talk to her," Itchy says.

"I talk to her all the time. That woman has heard more stories about my life than I've ever told a soul."

"She knows your fears? How you feel about this entire situation? How you feel about her?"

I lower my head, unable to look Kincaid in the eyes. He already knows the answers to that. I haven't been forthcoming with her. I haven't delved deep and gotten emotional. All of that was shit I didn't think she'd care about. I don't want to tell her that even though she's been terrified to leave my room that the last week or so has been the most relaxed I've felt in years. I don't want to force my own emotions and feelings on to her in fear that she won't feel the same or worse, that she'll act in the way she thinks I want her to rather than being her own person.

"You need to be real with her, Scooter." Dom's the master of sage advice.

"And as far as owning a woman not being your thing," Kincaid begins, "there's a difference in forcing someone to pretend to care for you. I own Emmalyn. Dom owns Makayla. Shadow owns Misty. Snatch and Itchy own each other. But our possession was earned through love and dedication, moral support and care. We own them and they own us back, and that proprietorship is what every single person walking this earth should work toward."

Well, when you put it that way...

"After you have a real talk with her, I think she would benefit from an appointment with Dr. Alverez. Griffin saw her for a while before he moved to Rhode Island. She's excellent in dealing with PTSD."

I nod at Shadow in agreement, but I know getting her to leave the property will be a challenge, especially after her failed attempt tonight.

Chapter 10

Mia

As if I'm still standing outside in the frigid air, I can't seem to get warm. Ryan walking away left me colder than the wind did when it pushed right against my skin as if I weren't wearing clothes at all.

I wanted a hot bath but couldn't convince myself I'd be okay without Ryan standing near the door or in the other room. That would leave only two doors between the outside world and me, so I changed clothes and climbed into his bed. Sinking into the middle of the mattress, wrapped in the sheets and blanket, surrounded by a half dozen pillows, still didn't bring enough warmth to keep my teeth from chattering.

He isn't gone long, maybe an hour at most, but when he returns, my cheeks heat in the darkness. I fully expected him to be out all night, meeting up with Kirsty or sleeping in the other room since he hated my kiss so much.

Tears sting my eyes as he walks through the room and into the bathroom. After a couple of minutes, he returns wearing sleep pants and a t-shirt, and as much as I want to look away, to pretend to be asleep, I can't seem to pull my eyes from him as he stands beside the bed, debating on whether or not he should join me.

Giving in, he huffs a sigh and climbs in on his side. I can tell he's doing his best not to touch me, but with his size and the fact that I'm lying in the center of the mattress, it's impossible.

The second his back hits the bottom sheet, I scoot closer, laying my hand on his stomach and my head on his chest.

A silent sob escapes my lips when he wraps his arm around my back and pulls me closer as if nothing horrible happened earlier. If I close my eyes and let my mind drift, I can imagine that he actually wants me here. I can picture him smiling at me when I wake up in his arms, rather than him being filled with the annoyance he's been so masterful at hiding.

His t-shirt is cool against my skin, but it's still warmer than I feel in my bones, so I get as close to him as I can manage.

"I'm sorry I kissed you." I swallow when my voice comes out husky and filled with emotion. "It's not fair to your girlfriend."

"I don't have a girlfriend, Sweet Mia."

"Are you engaged?" The words slip out of my mouth before I can stop them.

It's not a far-fetched conclusion. Technically, I guess I'm engaged too.

He laughs, low and gravelly, the action making my head shake on top of his chest. "Not engaged either."

"I heard your conversation earlier," I confess. "There's someone."

"What was going on between Kirsty and me wasn't serious."

Was? Wasn't?

Both are past tense, but I can't focus on how that makes me feel. Analyzing over that would only lead to a bigger mess in my head.

Silence fills the room, but just as I'm convinced he's fallen asleep he speaks again, "I loved kissing you."

My heart rate spikes, pounding against my ribcage so hard, I don't doubt he can feel it.

"But you kissed me for the wrong reasons."

I keep quiet, hoping he'll say more. It doesn't take long before my silence is rewarded.

"I'm sorry if I scared you. I was extremely upset that you put yourself in danger. And I can't promise that I won't respond that way again if you do something foolish, but I will never hurt you. I won't put my hands on you or force you to do anything. Never. That will never happen where I'm concerned. But if I get agitated again, you only have permission to touch me, to kiss me if you *want* to, not because of some attempt to get me to calm down. Do you understand?"

"I u-understand," I stammer.

He's exactly right. I pressed my lips to his because I saw it work back in Miami. Gabi, a girl that got there the same day I did, chose that tactic instead of fighting the guys. Last I saw of her, she was sitting on the leader's lap having a grand old time. I figured it wouldn't hurt to try the same approach with Ryan. He's right, most of me didn't want to kiss him, but even more of me doesn't want to lose him either. My selfish heart wants all of his time, all of his attention, and angry men don't stick around. Angry men stay late at the office and make lazy excuses for coming home half-drunk and smelling of cheap perfume.

I squeeze my eyes closed, convincing myself that Ryan and Jason are nothing alike, and if Ryan has a non-serious relationship with another woman, there's nothing I can do about that. It doesn't stop me from reminding myself that he's here with me and has been constantly since I was taken to the hospital.

He loved kissing me but stopped it because he was aware that I kissed him for the wrong reasons. I want to argue, now that I'm thinking about it. Most of me kissed him because of what he suspects, but there's a part of me that wanted to kiss him because he's helped me so much. I wanted to kiss him because it felt right. I wanted to kiss him because lying against him every day and not pressing my lips to his was driving me crazy.

I want to kiss him now, especially after he took a stand, even as a man and told me I can't kiss him unless it's for the right reasons. How idiotic of me to kiss him with his permission. What does that make me? Am I as bad as the men that pressed their disgusting lips to mine when I didn't want it? Did I take something from him he wasn't offering?

"Get out of your head," he whispers after a minute.

He chuckles and pulls me tighter against him, then his hand starts that soothing run down my back over and over.

"I like you, Mia. I think you're an amazing woman. I think you're a survivor and before long you'll be someone you can face in the mirror rather than avoiding it like you have been. I'm not one to give you the timetable on that type of recovery, but I'd be an asshole if I didn't tell you that we're leaving soon." I stiffen against his chest, but he keeps going on. "I'll have to leave for work. Sometimes that's three days, sometimes it's for weeks at a time. So I need you to work on being a little more independent, not because I'm rushing your recovery, but because I can't leave my focus here with you. Worrying whether you left the room to eat will put me in danger. What we do is serious shit, and it requires all of my attention."

I know he's telling the truth. Flashes of the men in their swat-like gear and assault rifles fills my head every time I close my eyes. Ryan and his guys were the saviors, but the men in the compound had guns just as big, and more than once I saw them turn those things on each other during an argument. Once, ten of us were forced to witness the massacre of three women on the front lawn.

"If you won't be comfortable here with the other women, then we need to start making arrangements to get you back home to your parents, or anywhere else you'll feel safe. I can't do my job if I think you're sneaking off in the middle of the night and freezing to death."

"What do you want?"

Asking the question brings a sense of foreboding, but if he's wanting to lay all the truth out right now, I need to do the very same.

"I want you safe. I want you happy."

"Where do you want me though?"

"If it were up to me, you'd be right here when I got back, but I can't be selfish. You aren't a prisoner here. I don't own you, and you don't owe anything to Cerberus. You tell me where you want to be and I'll make that happen, no questions asked."

I tangle my fingers in his t-shirt and let the tears of relief fall from my eyes and wet his shirt.

"Right here," I tell him. "I want to be right here."

Chapter 11

Scooter

Mia was missing less than a handful of hours, but Max won't even make eye contact with me. He hasn't said as much, but I'm certain he thinks I can't take care of his twin.

I'm not walking away from her, but at the end of the day I didn't ask for this job. She reached for me in the hospital and hasn't stopped since that moment.

Max acts like I took her from him, like I'm just as bad as the men that snatched her from the mall. I know he'll be involved in this latest mission to Venezuela, and then he'll go back wherever he came from. Maybe the absence of him constantly lingering around Mia will help her loosen up a little. She's always on edge no matter how much I tell her she's safe here. I think her brother watching her, expecting her to be okay immediately is too much pressure, and it's only setting her back.

"Let's get settled," Kincaid says as soon as he steps into the conference room. "We have a lot of things to discuss."

We situate ourselves around the table, waiting for news about deployment dates and details, but Shadow hasn't arrived yet. We never get started without him.

Tension and eagerness to be back at work fills the room as the guys enter and take their seats. We've been on leave for over a week, and it's easy to tell that the guys are chomping at the bit to get back to work. Time with family is nice, but we're all here for exactly this, the ability to help, the thrill of the ride, and this time around, the soul-deep desire to nail Cortez and Jiménez to the damn wall.

Coming in last, Shadow drops to his chair behind his computer and immediately begins to type onto his keyboard.

"We haven't spoken much about Blade," Kincaid begins once he has the entire room's full attention. "His biopsy came back, and although we're hopeful, the news isn't good."

"Fucking cancer," Kid hisses.

Blade has been the main guy filtering through the jobs that are presented to Cerberus. He navigates all the channels and sets everything up for us to make things go as smoothly as possible. He's imperative to the entire operation.

"He's going to have to take a step back," Kincaid continues. "They're going to start with chemo and as much as he assures me he can handle Cerberus and tend to his medical needs, I made the call that forces him to focus solely on his medical needs."

"I bet that didn't go over well," Snatch mutters.

Shadow grins. "He's pissed, to say the least."

Kincaid frowns at Shadow before turning back to us. "Hopefully, it's a temporary retirement, but in the meantime, we have someone that is capable of filling the shoes Blade leaves behind."

I stiffen when Max sits up straighter in his chair.

"Max worked for the CIA and is well versed in the tech Cerberus uses. He's been working with us this last week prepping for Venezuela. He's going to be taking over Blade's spot with the added benefit that he'll be here in New Mexico with us rather than all the way across the country."

"He's not a Marine," Jinx interrupts.

"It's true that a Cerberus has always required former enlistment, but times are changing," Dominic says. "Max is more than capable of handling what we need, and he's not going anywhere. Utilizing our resources comes ahead of anything else."

A couple of the guys around the table grumble, no doubt agitated at the hoops we had to jump through for consideration, and here it looks like Max just slid in at the right time with minimal experience.

Max's face is stoic the entire time this discussion is going on. He must've known that he would get pushback, but it doesn't seem to bother him. Tug doesn't open his mouth or give any of the guys voicing their opinions nasty looks. We're a team, and we've always been able to voice our concerns with no threat of reprisal. I'm glad to see that hasn't changed even when one of our guys is romantically involved with the focus of conversation.

"We leave for South America in three days," Shadow says, refocusing the group.

"Three days?" Rocker grumbles.

"Yes," Kincaid says. "We have a couple guys scouting for us, and we're still waiting to hear back from them. Both compounds have been reinforced. They've tripled security, but we think the added time over the holidays will make them grow lax. If anything, these guys like to party. Their constant consumption of alcohol and cocaine will take the edge off and make them sloppy."

"It's three more days for the women they have to get hurt. Three more days for them to get bored with what they have. Three more days for them to find new toys to play with," I hiss.

Three days would seem like a million years to anyone stuck in those compounds with them, getting hurt, abused, and tortured. Three days is three days too long.

"We have to wait for the intel," Shadow says after clearing his throat. "We understand that Mia makes this personal for several of you, but we won't be any good to other women like her if we rush in unprepared. This is the shortest time period we have that still keeps us safe."

I watch Max bite the inside of his cheek, and the sight of his slight head nod calms me some. I know he'd urge them to go in faster if that was a possibility. Mia is safe and I need to focus on that alone.

"We have confirmed... Max why don't you let everyone know what we have," Shadow urges.

"We have been able to confirm that Jiménez is in Venezuela. Some of the intel we're waiting on is to determine which compound he's at."

Shadow plugs something into his computer and the aerials of the two compounds fill the massive TV at the head of the room.

"Movement around the compounds are leading us to believe that they're joining forces, consolidating all into Xavier Cortez's place," Max continues. The screen flashes several times, revealing an increase of vehicles and supplies to the single compound.

"We'll still be hitting both even if intel comes back that Luis Cortez's property is empty. This is another reason for the delay. Having the split of men 70/30 to the different compounds is better than splitting it down the middle," Kincaid adds.

"And the Special Agent?" Grinch chimes in. "What's her status?"

"Special Agent Gabriella Butler is considered to have gone rogue," Dominic answers. "We've been keeping in touch with our contact at The Agency, and he's made it clear after some things have surfaced from Butler's past, they have no doubt she's been turned."

"She's not exactly been keeping a low profile either," Shadow mutters as pictures of a gorgeous woman flash on the screen. "This was taken yesterday."

"She's out fucking shopping?" I hiss when her smiling face fills the screen. The clothing racks in the background make it easy to determine what she's been up to.

"Are we sure she isn't still playing her part?" Jinx asks. "She's smiling and she left Miami before the raid with Jiménez, but couldn't she still be in survival mode?"

"The CIA won't disclose what they know that made them label her rogue, but they don't do that sort of thing lightly," Max interrupts. "They won't know for sure until they can get her back and debrief her."

"What does Mia say about Butler?" Rocker asks, looking in my direction.

Max is the one that growls, but I pay him no attention.

"Mia isn't in a place where she's able to help us with this," I spit.

"And we wouldn't ask that of her anyway," Kincaid says, taking a step closer to the table, a warning for all of us to keep our cool. "Abductee perceptions are always distorted and biased intel is dangerous for everyone involved."

"I didn't mean anything by it," Rocker grumbles. "I don't want to cause more problems than Mia already has."

I nod at my friend, my blood still boiling, hands still urging me to wrap them around his throat until he gives more than a half-assed apology.

"Intel is rolling in constantly. By the time we get to Venezuela, we'll be as prepared as we can be to make our moves on the compounds," Shadow says, redirecting our attention to where it needs to be.

"We're considering using an additional team, but we haven't pulled the trigger on that," Kincaid adds. "It's going to be all hands on deck."

My ears perk up with that news. We normally have one or two of the original guys join us on missions while the others stay behind and give direction via our headsets. Having them all head to South America with us makes it evident how important this is to the club.

"The Cortez brothers are responsible for over half of the trafficking coming out of Venezuela. We've worked dozens of cases that have them as the root of the problem. Luis Jiménez was responsible for a third of the cocaine being brought into Miami. Shutting these three guys down will have a huge effect on the sex trade as well as drugs," Shadow says as a few line graphs pop up on the screen. "The numbers are staggering, but if we manage to take them out and keep on the others that think they can pop up to fill those voids, we'll make it easier for the cleanup teams to keep a better handle on things moving forward."

"Max will stay behind here at the clubhouse," Kincaid continues. "Scooter?"

My head snaps up to my boss.

"We need you in the field, but we understand if you want to stay behind."

Max glares at me as if I'm the one who is asking to stay with Mia.

"I'm in, Prez." My knuckles crack as my fists clench. "I'm not missing this mission for anything."

Chapter 12

Mia

I want to be right here.

That's what I told Ryan last night before I drifted to sleep in his arms.

It was mostly the truth. I do want to be here. He swears I'm safe here, but the fear of being hurt again never leaves that dark little corner in the back of my head. I don't want to be on edge all the time. I'd rather my go-to expression was a smile like it used to be. I wish I wasn't wound so tight that I feel like I could pop open and explode any second.

I'm curled around myself, arms wrapped around knees pulled tight to my chest when I sense movement in the hallway.

Two guys walk by, so deep in conversation that they don't even look into the open doorway, then it swings open. Ryan's eyes flash when he sees me on the bed, and it's clear he thought he was going to find me gone again. I hate that I did that to him. Hate that I caused such an uproar that the entire group was out looking for me last night, but I don't think it'll happen again. Ryan assured me that I wasn't stepping on a girlfriend's toes by being here, but I don't think that's entirely true. He's gone from a life of freedom with the ability to do what he wants whenever he wants to staying in his room all day because it comforts me. He's bound to turn bitter about it, eventually.

"The door is open," Ryan says as he steps inside. He's winded, as if he left his meeting and ran down the hall to check on me.

I don't know whether I should be glad or irritated. I'm a little of both I guess.

"Keen eye, detective," I mutter.

I frown deeper with my failed attempt at a joke, but that doesn't keep the smile off his ruggedly handsome face.

"I figure it's the first step in doing things on my own," I explain when he stands in the center of the room, seemingly unsure of how he should act right now.

It's another thing I hate about this entire situation. He doesn't seem like the type that always second guesses his actions, but me being here is making him do just that. He's no longer sure of himself, but rather has to analyze each step to determine the best outcome.

"I think it's great. I was just—"

A knock at the door interrupts him, and he turns to see who's at his door.

"Hi," a girl chirps, and immediately my hackles go up.

Is this Kirsty?

"Hey, Jasmine," Ryan says in greeting. "What's up?"

Jasmine? Max mentioned Jasmine more than once during his long-winded, one-sided talks.

I lean to the side, wanting to get a look at the woman that has my brother tied up in knots. To be fair, Kingston shares a number one spot with this woman, too, according to my brother.

"I just came to bring Mia some things." Her soft voice is unassuming and filled with kindness.

"Mia?" Ryan turns back around, looking at me with questioning eyes. "Do you feel like company?"

His stance tells me that he'll fight her if he has to and the decision is all mine.

"Sure." I give him a smile that I hope he can't tell is fake. I'm curious about everyone else in the clubhouse, but at the same time, I've learned that just because it's a woman with a nice smile doesn't mean that they won't turn on you the first second they get. Women in the compound were mostly cutthroat, and they wouldn't have a problem putting a blade in your back if they thought it would help them somehow. That's what being there did. It turned us all into monsters.

Ryan takes a step to the right revealing a slender-framed woman with honey-brown hair, but he still keeps his position between the two of us. She smiles at me, the light catching the specks of amber in her mostly blue gaze.

"I'm Jasmine," she says in introduction, and like she's taken a class on how to deal with traumatized women, she doesn't offer her hand for me to shake.

I'm grateful because it keeps me from feeling like a jerk when I refuse.

"I'm Max's girlfriend." She grins. "I'm Max's and Kingston's girlfriend."

Her cheeks heat, turning the skin pink as if she's still a little embarrassed by the new relationship.

"Nice to meet you," I whisper.

Her head snaps back, and I know Max has told her that I don't speak, but I'm trying to stick to my New Year's resolution of interacting more.

"I brought you some things I thought you could use, but I want you to tell me to get lost if you feel like I'm pushing too much on you too soon."

"Are you pushy?" I blurt.

She grins as her shoulders lift. "Depends, I guess. I teach at the college, and young adults think everyone owes them something, so I guess at times I can be pushy, but that's not my intention with you."

She drops a duffel bag on the floor and crouches over it.

"I brought scarves." Like she's working with Mary Poppin's bag, she pulls at least a dozen brightly colored scarves from the bag and places them on the foot of the bed. "If you go outside again, I don't want your head to freeze."

I cringe at the idea that she's uncomfortable with my newly shaved head. It must be hard to ignore the woman who looks like a G.I. Jane reject, only I have all the injuries and none of the victory.

"I had to guess on your shoe size, so I left the tags on." Two boxes of shoes hit the bed next. "If they don't fit or if you hate them, just let me know and I can swing by after work tomorrow and exchange them. Let's see."

Jasmine continues to unload the bag, and I look up at Ryan. He's watching me, face unreadable, and I know he's trying to determine my mood before he responds to Jasmine and her offerings.

I give him a gentle smile to let him know I'm not going to freak out on my brother's girlfriend.

"Max got you a phone. He's already programed his number in." Jasmine looks up from the bag, handing Ryan the phone so he can hand it to me. "I will tell you that he urged me to ask you to call your parents, but I told him you'd do that when you were damn good and ready, but those numbers are in there as well."

"Thank you," I tell her with a genuine smile.

Ryan offers me the cell phone. I take it but immediately set it to the side.

"I brought a ridiculous stack of trashy magazines because I know sometimes you need to get lost in other people's bullshit while sorting through your own thoughts." She pulls at least a dozen magazines from the bag. "I recommend this top issue of Cosmo. It has a great article on the do's and don'ts of an amazing pedicure. It's my philosophy that if your feet feel great, you feel great."

She smiles up at me, and I find myself grinning back at her as well.

But then her face grows serious.

"He, umm—" Her eyes dart to Ryan, like she's going to ask advice about something, but then she smiles, resolved, and looks back at me. "He also got you a canister of pepper spray, a taser, and a 9mm."

My eyes widen as she spreads the items to the side of the magazines. They look completely out of place sitting beside the picture of the smiling women who is raving about the power of self-pleasure.

My eyes dart to Ryan, but his face is once again unreadable.

"If they make you feel safe, I want you to keep them," he tells me.

"You said I was safe here," I argue.

"You are safe here. I want you to feel safe," he clarifies. "If you don't and these things will help, I want you to keep them."

"I don't know how to shoot a gun."

"I can teach you gun safety."

"I'm somewhat of an expert myself," Jasmine interjects. "I can teach you a few things as well."

"I won't feel comfortable with them until I learn," I mutter.

"Not a problem." Jasmine pulls the gun from the comforter and shoves it back in the bag as if it being out of sight will make me forget the woman offered me a gun. "Still want to keep the pepper spray and the taser?"

I look back up at Ryan for answers, but he shakes his head. "This is your call. There isn't one person on this property that's going to cause you problems, but if you feel like you need them, then I want you to have them."

"I'm safe here," I tell him rather than ask. "But I may want them if we go somewhere."

A smile begins to pull up the corner of his mouth, but he catches it, schooling his face back to impassivity.

"Cool," Jasmine says as she stands. "We can just shove them in the closet until you leave the clubhouse."

She opens the closet door and stashes the pepper spray and taser in the top corner before turning back to her bag.

"I got you a couple pairs of fur-lined leggings. I have these in navy, and they are amazing." The bag continues to produce clothes and various items she thinks I need.

"I was going to go make us lunch," Ryan says, leaning over to whisper in my ear as Jasmine goes on and on about the body wash she pulls out next. "Do you want me to stay until she leaves?"

I shake my head, keeping my eyes on Jasmine as Ryan leaves the room.

"Good," she says when Ryan leaves the room.

My blood runs thin with her tone, but when I look back at her, she doesn't have a sinister look in her eyes. She has a box of tampons in her hand.

"Now that he's gone, we can do the girl talk stuff. I got you the multi-pack, but if you let me know what you prefer, I'll get you stocked up on those. I also got panty liners and regular pads."

"Thank you." My eyes burn with tears, but I do my best to hold them back. I'm so tired of crying.

She pulls a medium-sized pouch from the bag.

"Don't take this as me telling you that you need any of this shit, but I just wanted it available if you want it." She hands me the bag, and it's the first time she's directly offered me something. I take it on instinct. "There's a little makeup in there, but there're also some face creams. There's Chapstick and cuticle cream. I tossed in a couple samples of shampoos and conditioners that people rave about helping hair grow."

I watch her face, and although I can see concern in her eyes, what I don't see is pity. I know I still have yellowing bruises on my face, but she isn't focusing on any of that. She's here to help, and she makes no apologies for that.

"This is more than just because you're my brother's girlfriend," I say, my eyes searching hers.

"I was adopted by my older sister and Dominic. He's the club president's older brother," she begins. "When I was younger, before Cerberus welcomed me with open arms, I lived with the Renegade MC. Those guys were awful. They hurt people. Hell, they hurt each other just for the thrill of it. I've seen women get hurt and abused. I was a coward then. I didn't help. I stayed out of the way and huddled in the corner. I knew my time was coming soon. I felt the men's eyes on me. Could almost read their filthy thoughts."

She shakes her head violently as if trying to dispel the vulgar thoughts.

"How old were you?"

"Eight when Dominic and Makayla got together."

"You were a child not a coward."

She swallows as she stands, making her way closer to me. "And you were a woman overpowered by men who have spent their lives perfecting the ability to take women and hurt them. What happened to you wasn't your fault, either."

She places her hand on my knee, giving it a slight squeeze.

"Everyone will tell you to get better, to put it behind you, but until you forgive yourself for the things that were always out of your control, you'll never be able to move forward. Start there, first."

Chapter 13

Scooter

"A week tops," Jinx assures me as I take a loaf of bread from his hand.

"I don't know, man. I think we'll be gone longer than that," Grinch adds. "They still haven't found Caroline Spring."

Caroline was one of the three girls we went after the last time we were in Venezuela raiding Xavier's compound. The youngest girl, eleven-year-old Lupe was found deceased. Caroline's mission buddy, Maria Yves, the girl she was abducted with, was rescued.

"It's possible she was moved to the other Cortez compound," I remind them. "Hitting them both at the same time means we'll clear everyone out, but that's a lot to coordinate, and I know it'll take longer than a week."

"They're constantly working on it," Jinx tells me with a brotherly slap to the back. "Just because we're not there doesn't mean the work isn't getting done. All we'll have to do is show up, infiltrate, and fucking kill them all."

A throat clearing across the room halts all conversation. We're usually pretty good about only talking about work when it's just us guys. The meetings are great but sometimes we have to step away for a while before we can process the information we've been given.

Jasmine is standing in the doorway of the kitchen and knowing that she's left my room makes me work faster on Mia's and my lunch, but before I can turn back to the ham and cheese sandwiches, Jasmine steps aside and Mia is standing there with her.

She's changed out of my baggy sweats into a pair of form fitting leggings that hug her from the knee down. The top half of her legs are still covered with one of my t-shirts, and it makes me grin that she's still in some of my clothes.

"Ham and cheese okay?" I ask, rather than making it known how excited I am that she's out of the room.

We tried this yesterday, and it ended with her taking off. I vow not to let that happen again today.

She nods, smiling at me before letting her eyes wander around to all the guys in the kitchen. They part, giving her room as Jasmine leads her to the furthest table in the corner. Mia sits with her back to the wall, facing all the guys, and without a word the men move around, each helping her in any way they can.

Jinx grabs a canned soda from the fridge and places it in front of her on the table, all the while keeping as much distance as possible.

Rocker grabs several different kinds of chips and two different flavors of dips, and he also places them on her table. He also whispers an apology for walking into the kitchen yesterday without a shirt on, then pledges to never do that again.

Grinch, weirdly named such because he loves listening to Christmas music year-round, grabs glasses for her and Jasmine both and fills them with ice.

"Can you get me a glass of ice?" I teasingly ask Grinch.

"Get it yourself you lazy fucker," he responds.

Mia freezes, but when Jasmine leans closer to her ear and whispers something, she slowly begins to relax.

"They're barbarians," Jasmine mutters as I hand Mia the plate with her sandwich on it. "But they're mostly housebroken."

A small smile plays on my girl's lips as she takes the plate.

"I'm completely housebroken," I tell her before stepping a way to finish my sandwich.

"Lies," Tug says as he walks in the room.

He's mindful of Mia's space, but it doesn't stop him from swiftly crossing the room and planting his lips on Jasmine's mouth.

Mia watches them as they kiss and whisper to each other, but she doesn't seem adversely affected by it. When Max enters next and does the exact same thing, her cute little nose scrunches up at the sight of her brother kissing someone. I chuckle, topping my massive sandwich with the second piece of bread before joining them at the table.

Tug and Max are opposite of Mia and Jasmine, so I sit on Mia's left side.

"Did you want extra pickles this time?" I whisper in her ear.

"This is perfect," she answers, her fingers toying with the corner of her bread. She's yet to take a bite.

"We can eat in the bedroom if you're more comfortable there," I offer.

"I'm okay." Her lips pull up in a quick smile, but it's gone in a blink.

I know she can feel Max's eyes on her. Hell, I feel like they're boring a hole in both of us right now, but neither of us acknowledge him.

She's dealing with his resurrection on top of her abduction, and I don't think she knows how to process the two events individually much less at the same time.

"French onion or cheese?"

"What?" Mia turns in my direction. Her cheeks are flushed and her breathing has grown more rapid.

"Dip for your chips?" I point at the spread in front of her, but I don't think the distraction is going to work.

"No thank you," she mutters, keeping her eyes down on her sandwich.

"I think we have bean dip in the fridge." Pressing my hands to the table to stand, I'm stopped by Mia's hand on my arm.

When I look down, her eyes are begging me not to leave.

"I'll get it," Jasmine offers and it only take a handful of seconds before she's back, scooping some of the dip out of the container and placing it on Mia's plate.

Mia whispers a thank you, but I don't think she's going to eat a thing. There's too much going on, too many people pulling her attention away from her meal. I'm seconds away from asking her again if she wants to leave, but she finally picks up her sandwich and takes a bite.

She moans into her food. I've learned that ham and cheese is her favorite, and I'll keep making it for her until she tells me she's sick of it. In the hospital, I was worried she'd waste away to nothing. It's why I started hand feeding her soup when they brought it to the room.

Eventually, the other guys finish their lunches and begin to filter out of the room. As each one leaves, she grows calmer. Her muscles relax and the steel rod forming her spine begins to soften a little.

Max shows no sign of leaving. Nor does Jasmine or Tug.

Before long, we're the only five people left in the kitchen dining area, and even though Max, Tug, and Jasmine carry on an unassuming conversation, they don't attempt to force Mia into their chat.

But it only lasts so long.

"I'm Kingston," Tug says as he offers his hand across the table.

Mia looks at it before darting her eyes first to mine and then to her brother. Neither one of us urges her to take his hand. I don't know about Max, but I don't want her to feel obligated to touch anyone she doesn't want to.

With a weak smile and slow movements, Mia shakes his hand, but she pulls it back quickly.

"I'm…" My friend, and fellow Cerberus teammate looks between the man at his side and the woman across from him, and the love in his eyes for both is as clear as day. "I'm theirs."

"I remember you, idiot," Mia chuckles.

My body freezes. I haven't heard her laugh at all, but even her chuckles are few and far between since we met.

"Just trying to break the ice. You can cut the tension with a fucking knife in here." Tug gives her a smile that I have no doubt has stopped a lot of women in their tracks. Men, too, now that I'm thinking about it. "I'm really glad you're safe, Pia."

Max's eyes go wide, and I think he's about ready to throw down with his lover, but Mia chuckles again. Twice in less than five minutes? Is the world coming to an end?

"Really?" she playfully snaps at Tug. "I'm not twelve anymore. I think we're all old enough to have a conversation without resorting to childhood nicknames."

"Pia?" Jasmine asks as she lifts a chip to her mouth.

"Mia Pia," my girl mumbles. "They were so mean to me as a kid."

"Mean?" Max says with a grin. "You're the one that couldn't take a hint. You followed us everywhere."

Mia glares at her brother, but I can tell by the sparkle in her eyes I've never seen before that she's not angry with him.

"I followed you around because I was bored, and because maybe I had a crush on Kingston." Her cheeks grow redder with the confession.

"Well," Max chuckles, "apparently, so did I."

We all laugh at that, and the smile doesn't leave my face as I watch them all interact.

She hasn't been this light or talkative. It's amazing, but I also can't help but wonder how long it will last. I think she's happy, but I can't judge the genuineness in her smile either.

It doesn't take long for the sparkle to begin to dim, and it's as if the others at the table can sense her retreat back into herself. Jasmine stands, offering to clean up the kitchen and her two men stay behind to help as we make our way out.

Once in the safety of my room, I feel like I can breathe a little better. She didn't insist on going to her room, and she doesn't have that look in her eye that says she wants to bolt.

She doesn't make a move to climb into the bed. She just stands in the middle of the room and eyes it warily.

"What's wrong?" I inch closer, but at the same time keep distance between the two of us.

It's one of the hardest things I've ever done. It's difficult to keep my own needs in check. She gravitated to me because she feels like I can protect her. I'm her savior, the man who carried her out of hell, but at the same time, I need to give her room to heal, and forcing my needs on her, the need to touch her, to tell her everything will be fine, to make her yearn for my warmth the way I yearn for hers is selfish. It can also be detrimental to her recovery. She has to set the pace and direction here.

"I feel like I'm disrupting your entire life."

"You are," I tell her honestly.

She jerks, her body stiffening as she looks up at me.

"Before you, I'd never lie in bed all day and watch movies. Before you, I wouldn't be caught dead sleeping in clothes." I wink at her with this information, but she isn't seeing the playfulness I'm trying to display. "Mia Vazquez, you've turned my entire world upside down. I've gone on countless missions. Protected my country for years in the Marine Corps, and then you came along, making me feel legitimately useful for the first time in my entire life. I want to lie in bed with you and watch movies all day, if that's what you want."

"Next are you going to tell me that you like wearing clothes to bed now?" She rolls her eyes but the apprehension that was clouding her eyes is beginning to lift.

"I like sleeping with you against me. I like wrapping my arms around you in the middle of the night and listening to you sigh as you settle against my chest." I grin, deciding to test the waters. "Would I like to do that without clothes on? You bet, but that may never happen."

Her face falls, and I can't believe how much I'm fucking this up.

"What I'm trying to tell you, Sweet Mia, is that you're under no obligation to reciprocate anything where I'm concerned. You don't have to kiss me or touch me or placate me in any way as payment for the kindness I've offered to you. You don't owe me anything. You don't owe Cerberus anything. As far as you and me? This goes where *you* want it to go, not where I hope it will."

"What do you want to do right now?" she asks with a yawn.

It's clear what she wants, but at the same time, I'm sticking to my word about not pushing her.

"Whatever you want," I tell her with a grin. "I'm leaving in three days."

This isn't news to her. We discussed it last night, but now there's a timetable to attach to that news.

"Three?" As she looks up at me her eyelashes brim with tears.

"Yeah, and it'll take a lot of energy, so I'm hoping you don't suggest running a marathon right now."

She chuckles, but it's not light and airy like it was in the kitchen earlier.

"I'd like to take a nap," she says softly.

I'm kicking off my boots before she can even climb into the bed.

Chapter 14

Mia

Ryan leaves for Venezuela tomorrow. We've spent the last two days watching Lost on Hulu, and it's been easy enough to lose myself in the TV drama, but as the clock ticks by, the more nervous I grow. Like a fool, I slept in my own room last night, and even though it's only early afternoon, my eyes are heavy with the need for sleep. Every sound in the clubhouse woke me up, and I'm sure I spent more time staring at the ceiling trying to convince myself not to go to Ryan's room than I did actually resting.

Max will be the only man left behind. All others are leaving the country to try and track down the man responsible for my abduction. I'm not delusional. I know that Luis Jiménez has hurt countless women and will continue to do so if someone doesn't stop him. Their mission isn't just about me, but it eases me some to know that they'll make sure he can't hurt another person.

For some reason, I'm apprehensive with the Cerberus men here, but the thought of them all being gone also causes me concern, and I hate that I want both things, and can have neither.

All of my meals have been spent outside of the room since lunch the other day with Jasmine. Since they live in houses behind the clubhouse, I haven't seen Emmalyn, Misty, and Khloe much, but Ryan assures me they'll be around more when the farting, grunting, stinky guys are gone—his explanation, not mine. They've been incredibly nice and welcoming the times that we did interact.

I was a fool to think I'd have three solid days to spend with Ryan before he left. He's been in and out today, some time spent in meetings, some time spent at Kincaid's house.

Right now, they're all in that big meeting room in the center of the clubhouse and have been locked away for the last hour.

"Mia?"

Startled, I turn too quickly in the direction of the voice and manage to drop my bottle of water.

It skitters across the floor, rolling until it stops against the toe of Camryn Davison's shoe.

"Still jumpy?" she asks with a smile as she bends to pick up my bottle.

"Most days," I mutter as she hands the water back to me.

"The offer still stands for the anxiety meds." I met Camryn the day after I left the clubhouse and nearly froze to death walking away from this place.

"I don't want meds." Some of the girls were forced to take all sorts of things. Prescription meds, illicit drugs, bottle after bottle of liquor were forced down their throats. I was one of the lucky ones, and the guys who fancied me weren't into sedation. No, they loved to hear me scream, wanted me to be able to fight them. Conquering me was their biggest thrill.

"Okay. Just thought I'd offer. Let me know if you change your mind. How is that pinky toe doing?"

The only concern I had after Ryan found me and brought me back here was the smallest toe on my right foot. It took forever before I got feeling back in it. The following morning when I got into the shower, it felt like fire was set to it when the warm water touched it.

"It's better. Full feeling. No longer hurts."

"Good. Good." Her eyes rake up and down my frame, but I can tell she's assessing me medically, not sizing me up to sell me to her pimp, which I was certain she was doing the first time we met.

Loud conversation drifts through the double doors of the big conference room, and Camryn takes a step closer.

"How are you sleeping?"

"Better," I answer honestly.

"The guys are leaving tomorrow. How will you sleep then?"

My jaw snaps shut, but even several years younger than I am, she gives me that doctor look, and I open my mouth to answer. It's the fear or missing him that worries me the most. I've mostly accepted that I'm safe here but being wrapped in Ryan's arms at night keeps the demons that try to haunt me at bay.

"I don't know. Terribly, I imagine," I finally respond.

"I can—"

I jerk my hand up to silence her. "I don't want any pills."

She gives me a sad smile. "I was going to suggest warm tea before bed. Focused calming breaths and meditation would help, too."

"Okay."

We chat a little longer, but eventually she excuses herself and leaves. Stressed, thinking about Ryan leaving, I head back to his room and crash on the bed. The cell phone Jasmine gave me several days ago taunts me from the bedside table.

Sighing after staring at the innocuous thing like it contains the plague, I pick up and resign myself to making the call I've avoided since I arrived in New Mexico.

I expect the call to go to voicemail because everyone, even my parents, screen their calls now, but my mother picks up after the first ring. So much for a few more minutes of avoidance.

"Mia?" My mother's hope-filled voice comes across the line.

"It's me, Ma. How are you?"

Max must've given them this phone number.

"I'm more worried about you, *mi amor*."

I sigh, unable to hide my overwhelming thoughts. I love my parents. I truly do, but with everything that has happened to me, I don't feel like the same person. Their little girl was beaten and raped out of me over the course of the seven weeks I was in captivity. Before answering, I wonder if I even deserve their love. Could I have done more to protect myself, short of not walking away with the stranger in the parking lot? Could I have protected myself better after they locked me in that tiny room with those other women?

"I'm okay, Ma. How's Pa?"

"He's fine. Worried about you. It's been so long since we heard your voice. We miss you dearly."

"I miss you, too," I tell her, and that's the truth.

I miss Sunday dinners.

I miss smiling as my mother frets around the kitchen making sure everything is right as if a celebrity is coming to share a meal rather than just family.

I miss how easy it was to get out of bed back then.

I miss being able to walk around without the fear of being hurt.

I miss a million things, a million things I don't feel like I'll ever get back.

"Jason misses you, too."

I should feel something with the mention of my fiancé. I should miss him the most, right?

I feel nothing. There's an empty void inside of me, with no room left for him, and that makes me feel something dark, akin to self-hatred because even though Jason is the one I promised to marry, it's Ryan that I picture when I think of more, when I think of a future.

"Jason hasn't tried to contact me. He hasn't called or sent messages through Max." I don't honestly know about the latter part of my statement, but I figure my brother would say something if Jason reached out to him.

"He's a very busy man, Mia."

It takes all I have not to huff my indignation into the phone. I haven't been Jason's number one in a very long time, so I shouldn't be surprised with his lack of communication, but I imagine that most people would drop everything they're doing to love and comfort someone who has been through what I've been through.

"Yes, well..." I don't know what else to say about it. The issue is between Jason and me. My mother likes to meddle, and I learned long ago that coming to her to discuss issues about my fiancé only makes her remind me how important the man is in a family. My parents were born in Mexico, and they brought their old ways to Louisiana with them when the immigrated.

"When should we expect you home? Soon I hope."

"I don't know honestly. I like it here."

Here isn't there. Here isn't where I was taken. I think I need the separation to maintain the miniscule amount of safety I feel being so far away. Plus, what do I have to go back to other than prying parents who want to shove me into the arms of a man that loves his fast-track responsibility to partnership rather than the woman he swore he wanted to have babies with?

"I have to go, Ma. I'll call again soon."

I hang up the phone before she can hear the lie in my tone.

I don't get long to stew in my thoughts because a knock on the door echoes through the room. It's cracked open, and for the very first time since I arrived, I don't begin to freak out when it's pushed open.

"Mia?" Emmalyn, the president's wife sticks her head inside but makes no move to come in. "I was hoping you'd help me make lunch for the guys. They've been in meetings all day, and they're going to be starving when Diego finally cuts them loose."

"Sure," I answer, even though I know I'll do my best to be gone from the room when they begin to file out of the conference room.

Misty and Khloe are also in the kitchen with a spread of ingredients in front of them by the time Emmalyn and I make it into the room.

"We're making enchiladas," Khloe says with a soft smile. "It's the easiest way to feed all of them at one time."

"The fastest, too," Misty adds as she pops the top off of a rotisserie chicken. "They think it's gourmet food, when really it's the simplest thing. Do you want to help me with the chicken?"

"Sure," I tell her as I step up to the sink to wash my hands.

Soft country music plays in the background as we work. Misty and I pull the meat off the chickens while Emmalyn and Khloe get the sauce and tortillas ready.

In less than an hour, we have six pans of enchiladas baking in the oven and more rice and beans than I've ever seen, which is saying something considering my nationality.

Noise from the conference room drifts into the kitchen, and I'm seconds away from making an excuse to leave when a man covered in tattoos enters the room. He's got stars tattooed on his face with little sparkling studs in the center, and his neck and hands are covered in ink. Months ago, I wouldn't have given him a second look. Tattoos are so commonplace where I'm from, but they were rampant among the men in Miami, too.

"This is Jaxson," Emmalyn says so close to my ear that I jump, startled that I was so focused on him that I didn't even sense her approaching me. "He's married to Rob. Samson, whom you've met is his son. Delilah is Samson's twin. You'll meet her during spring break."

Jaxson smiles at me, but like many of the other men here at the clubhouse, he doesn't offer his hand or invade my space.

Another man, one with a long beard and kind eyes enters behind the tattooed man, and as crazy as it seems, when he leans over and plants a kiss on the star tattoo, it makes me feel more relaxed.

"I'm Rob," the new arrival says, also keeping his distance. "Are you responsible for the amazing smells coming from the room?"

"I h-helped," I tell them both, still leery of them even though they're being nice. There were guys that seemed nice back at the compound, too, and that didn't stop them from taking what I wasn't offering.

Chapter 15

Scooter

I know Mia needs her independence. Her choosing to sleep in her own room is a step in that direction, and I imagine it's been hard fought, but that still doesn't keep me from missing her warmth on my side or the sweet smell of her hair. My fingers itch to run up and down her spine, to tell her more stories about my life.

She stayed alone last night, and this evening, she went that direction again. Emmalyn said she helped make lunch for all of us, but by the time I made it to the kitchen, she was already gone. It took as much resistance as I could muster to not got to her and make sure she was okay.

The afternoon was filled with even more meetings as we gear up to head to South America. I've been with Cerberus for years, and I don't think I've ever participated on a mission of this caliber. Sure, every job is important, but there're a lot of cogs in this machine, a lot riding on our success, and it's making everyone hyper focused.

Preparation for these types of jobs takes the longest. The mission, once we hit the property actually goes by very quickly. It's a slow buildup to the rush of adrenaline we get to cash in on the day of infiltration, which is over in a matter of minutes most times. I live for that rush. Live for the blitz of endorphins that makes me feel as powerful as a god, unstoppable and ferocious. It's the sole reason I joined Cerberus in the first place.

This next mission is different. Venezuela and defeating both the Cortez brothers and Luis Jiménez is now personal. Their demise holds more meaning than the thrill that comes with taking down a terror cell. Their destruction will give Mia some of her power back. It'll let her feel just a little safer in her own skin, and that's what's most important to me.

Like a ton of bricks slamming into my chest, I gasp when my next thought filters in.

I love her. I fucking love Mia Vazquez.

And that's wrong on so many levels.

She's engaged to another man.

She's been hurt, probably beyond my wildest imagination, which is saying a lot considering my line of work.

She trusts me to protect her, and I'm going to fuck it all up by letting my feelings get in the way.

She clings to me for safety because she knows I won't let anyone hurt her, and somehow my body and mind has distorted all of that until I convinced myself that she's mine, that she feels the same way about me that I feel for her.

I don't do love.

I don't do attachments.

I don't let a single woman invade my every thought.

Yet, Mia's there. In my head. In my heart. In my fucking soul.

This is bad, so terribly bad.

This can't end well.

My pulse is racing with my realization when my bedroom door creaks open. Mia appears, looking like an angel, backlit with the light of the hallway surrounding her. She steps in, closing the door and once again wrapping us in darkness, but she doesn't climb in the bed with me.

Now would be the perfect time to urge her back to her room, to tell her that she's doing good, and her independence is what she needs. I could remind her that she survived one night in there, and she needs to keep that momentum.

I watch her as she stands beside the bed biting her thumb nail.

I need to ask her to leave because if I do what my body and heart are begging me to do, she's going to discover my secret, and that will ruin everything. My true feelings have the power to ruin the platonic relationship we've been building. She'll no longer feel safe. The expectancy that comes along with being in love with someone will eat away at what we've built like acid until there's nothing left.

I don't listen to my head because my body craves her touch. Without a word, I lift the edge of the blankets and sigh with contentment as she settles on my chest. I do my best to ignore my throbbing cock as her heat engulfs me. He'll only complicate things.

Her fingers tangle in my t-shirt, and I pat myself on the back for wearing clothes to bed. Before her, I didn't, and even though she didn't come in here last night, I crawled in bed this evening hoping that tonight would be different.

My eyes drift closed, content as I've ever been, but she startles me when she begins to speak.

"Sephora was having a lipstick sale that day," she whispers.

I know what day she's talking about. She's never once breathed a detail about what happened the day she was abducted. I never asked and figured she'd talk when she was ready, if that day ever came. It seems we've arrived, and it truly sucks that it's the day before I have to leave her for who knows how long. Setbacks usually come at the tail end of these types of conversations, and I won't be here to hold her when they do.

She huffs a humorless laugh against my chest, and I hate that I can't feel her warm breath on my skin. I hold her closer, encouraging her to go on without using words.

"Vanity put me in the crosshairs of evil. I wasn't even out of lipstick. I just wanted more and saving money was a good enough excuse as any. The guy in the parking lot was clean-cut, handsome, and unassuming. He said he had car trouble, and his cell phone was dead. I offered to let him use mine, and when he said he had to get his address book out of his glove box, I didn't think anything of it. I should've seen the signs. I mean, what guy in his mid-twenties even has an address book. We live and die by our phones. But he was dressed nice, and he smiled at me like I was the prettiest girl in the world." She swallows so hard, I can hear her throat work. "Jason hadn't smiled at me like that for longer than I can remember."

I hate even the mention of the fiancé waiting for her back home, not that he's made much of an effort to get her back. Broken women take time and understanding, and even though I didn't technically meet him at the hospital, my first impression of him didn't lead me to believe he had the patience for the work it would take. No, he seems like the guy that will show back up once she's already been put back together.

"The attention was nice. He flirted with me, and I thought it was harmless. Just a little fun, a few minutes of joy before I walked away and went back home to Jason, but then we neared his car. The pinch in my neck wasn't even that much of a concern. Louisiana is filled with mosquitos and that's about what it felt like, but then I saw him pulling the needle away, and my first thought was this cute guy is kind of a jerk. Even as my arms and legs grew sluggish, I never imagined that he was taking me. I never thought that I'd be gone for seven weeks."

Tears wet my shirt, and I flex my arm around her middle, knowing that if I hold her any tighter against me, she'll find it difficult to breathe.

"The bag he put over my head smelled of defeat, and when I woke in the trunk of the car hours later, I knew I wasn't the first one to wear it. I wasn't the first woman this handsome smiling man drugged and abducted. I didn't know where we were going or how long I would be there, but I knew I was going to be raped. I knew that men who took girls used them in the most degrading ways, and I swore in the trunk of that car that I'd fight them every step of the way. If they killed me, I could die knowing that I was strong even if they were stronger. I may lose my dignity, but I wouldn't lose my will to live."

She grows silent as sobs shake her entire body. I don't whisper to her. I don't promise her that everything will be okay. I don't know that they will. Her body is healing rapidly from what they did to her, but it's the mind that takes the longest. And sometimes the trauma is just too much to fully overcome.

"But I did." She cries harder. "I lost that will to live, and I prayed to God to come take me. I offered my soul to the devil, just knowing that hell would be easier to endure than the nightmare I was living on earth."

I rest my chin on the top of her head as my hand begins the slow glide up and down her back.

"Then the door to the room opened, and I vowed to push the next man to his breaking point. I knew the next time would be the last time because I would force him to kill me. It had to end. I was done being their victim. But it was you who walked into the room that day. It wasn't the man with the scars on his face or the man with the tattoo on the back of his hand who liked me to fight him. It was you. You saved me that day."

I open my mouth to tell her that I'm only one piece in a massive machine that was working that day, but I can't. I want to be her savior. I want to be the man she always comes to when she's scared, lonely, or when she just needs someone to hold her.

I *need* to be that person for her, for me.

"I know you're leaving tomorrow, but I just wanted you to know that no matter what, even if you can't take down those evil men, you saved me, and for that I'll always be grateful."

With tears staining her face, Mia raises her head and presses her lips to mine. Softened by her crying, her mouth is pure perfection, but this kiss is nothing like the one she tried to wield against me when she thought I was angry. This kiss is sweet and tender, a salty reminder of the woman she was, and it's filled with the promise of the woman she hopes she'll be again one day.

It's over way too soon, but then she brushes her fingers down my cheek while looking into my eyes, and I'm lost to her. I'm lost in her pain, in the prospect of her future happiness, and now I'm the one making vows, promising my soul to whichever entity will take it if it means I can spend my life with this amazing woman.

"Just make sure you come back to me."

I nod my head without even thinking.

Even death couldn't keep me away from her at this point.

"I promise."

Her lips press to mine one last time before she settles back on my chest. She drifts to sleep quickly, while I lie awake and imagine a life I never even dreamed of before.

Chapter 16

Mia

My confessions last night drained me, but the benefit of that is I slept like the dead.

But when I wake, Ryan is gone, the side of his bed cold, revealing that he'd been missing a while.

Anxiety tries to take over, but I push it down and stand.

Doubt that I can survive without him tries to seep in as I shower for the first time without him standing sentry at the door, but I manage to shove that down as well.

Just like I'd grown tired of being hurt while at the compound, I've also grown weary of letting my racing thoughts and fear control me. I'm safe here. I know that. I've known it since the first time I stepped foot on the property, probably since Ryan scooped me up off the floor in Miami, but only now, am I actually letting myself believe it. I have to. Living in fear is no longer an option. If I want my life back, I have to fight for it, and that's exactly what I plan to do.

A knock and voices down the hall don't make my skin crawl like it once did, but I'd be lying to myself if I didn't acknowledge the increase of my pulse.

"Mia?" a female voice says on the other side of Ryan's bedroom door. "Are you awake?"

The question is followed by a knock, and even though I want to be alone, I open the door, knowing that I've had enough solitude the last two weeks to last a lifetime.

Misty smiles at me from the hallway, and even though she's only like ten years younger than my own mother, I feel like we could be friends, and I need as many friends as I can get since Ryan will be gone for an undisclosed amount of time.

"Hey," I offer because I'm unable to think of anything else to say.

"We were having breakfast and coffee at Em's. Want to join us?"

"Sure," I answer before I can even think about telling her no.

Misty waits for me to grab one of Ryan's oversized hoodies since we have to leave the clubhouse to get to Emmalyn's home. I blame the frigid cold for the way my body shakes and shivers as we take the kitchen exit, but it continues as we step inside of the magnificent home.

"Wow," I mumble as we enter through the kitchen of Em's house. "And I thought the kitchen in the clubhouse was huge."

"We do most of the family stuff here," Misty explains as she shrugs out of her jacket.

I opt to keep Ryan's sweatshirt on, certain I'll never get warm again even as heat surrounds me.

"Even as big as it is, it still gets crowded when all the kids are home from college," Khloe says as she joins us in the kitchen.

The luxurious scent of coffee and sweets fill the air as we step closer to the kitchen island. Before long, Emmalyn joins us with a smile on her face.

"Now that the men are gone, we can talk freely," she says, pouring four steaming cups of coffee.

This was a bad idea. They want to talk freely? It took everything I had to make my whispered confessions in the dark last night, and even though I've grown closer to Ryan with each passing day, it was one of the most difficult things I've ever done. I can't discuss the same things with the women. As nice as they seem, I don't have a bond or connection to them like I do with Ryan.

"I would never tell Dustin this," Khloe begins, "but I'm bored beyond belief, and even though it's only been six months, I regret retiring."

"Me too," Em adds. "There's only so much I can find to keep myself busy."

"What did you both do?" I ask, hoping that the topic of conversation stays on them and doesn't begin to veer to me.

"I taught elementary school," Em says before hitching a thumb over her shoulder to indicate Khloe. "She was braver and taught middle school."

I look at Misty, who just shrugs. "I've always stayed home. I don't have a problem with boredom. That's what naps and books are for."

Emmalyn scoffs and Khloe chuckles.

"We're used to chaos, but since Landon is older now, I can't seem to find anything that holds my interest. He's so wrapped up in sports and his friends at school," Khloe explains.

"Don't forget his recent discovery of the opposite sex," Emmalyn interjects.

They all chuckle, and I find myself smiling, too.

"And there's that." Khloe smiles. "I miss the baby days when the entire daylight hours were spent making them meals, cleaning up after them, and providing for their every need."

"I don't," Misty huffs. "Griffin and Cannon were a damn handful. Hell, Cannon is still a handful, and he's a grown man."

"I'm a grandma," Emmalyn says with a smile. "That's what you ladies need. Grandbabies."

Khloe takes a step back, waving her arms in front of her. "I think I'm a couple years away from that stage."

"Ivy has to finish school, and I'm pretty sure they're enjoying their alone time together. Cannon? Well, with the way that boy behaves, I wouldn't be surprised if we had babies show up on the doorstep."

"Ivy is your daughter?" I ask Emmalyn.

She nods.

"And Griffin is my son," Misty adds. "And when they get married, we'll truly be family."

"Do you want children?" Khloe asks as she blows the top of her coffee.

"I did," I answer honestly. "Now, I can't even think about—"

I frown as I look at them.

"Now I don't know," I rush out.

"You'll know when you're ready." Emmalyn sets down her coffee cup as she stands. "How about we have some real fun?"

Misty groans, but she stands as well. We all follow Emmalyn through her house, and seconds later we're stepping into a craft room that would rival anything Martha Stewart could imagine.

"Holy crap," I mutter as I step inside.

The walls are lined with shelves filled with canisters of different crafting materials. The far-right corner is a sewing station with four different types of machines.

"I can never stick to one thing at a time," Emmalyn confesses as she walks toward the huge table in the center of the room.

"Last month it was quilts and learning to knit," Misty whispers, but she keeps her voice loud enough for everyone to hear. "Now she swears this diamond painting mess is relaxing. I find it only hurts my eyes and makes me feel twenty years older than I actually am."

"Diamond painting?" I ask. How rich are these people?

"Diamond painting," Khloe confirms. "And it is very relaxing."

She points to a canvas with color coded little squares all over it.

"These are called drills." Emmalyn points to several baggies with tiny pieces of plastic in them. "It's sort of like paint by numbers, but it's 3D and the end product is magnificent."

"So you've heard," Misty interrupts her friend before turning back to look at me. "She hasn't actually finished one yet."

"We just got started," Khloe says in defense of herself and her friend. "It's going to be amazing."

"Interested?" Emmalyn asks as hope fills her eyes.

"A nap would be better," Misty mumbles. "Or that book I was telling you girls about."

"My entire life is a fairy-tale," Emmalyn says with sparkles in her eyes. "I don't need to read about a happily ever after when I'm in the middle of my own."

Misty shrugs, and it seems she can't argue it either way. Not for her friend or for herself.

I try not to feel bitter. I try not to judge them for the things I've suffered. I wouldn't wish what happened to me on another living soul, but not everyone lives a fantasy. Not everyone gets to have a fairy-tale happily ever after. Some people are hurt and broken. Some people fight demons daily, never knowing if they will overcome them at all.

I take a deep breath, resigning myself to spending time with these women even though I feel even more like the odd man out. I try not to feel like the charity case, like the lost girl who needs attention.

I pull up a stool, with my opinions changing of these women, and start to attach the little plastic pieces to the sticky canvas. I can't be friends with them, no matter how genuine their smiles.

I'm pitying myself and hating that I'm here in their perfect world and in their perfect house with thoughts of their perfect husbands filling my brain when Emmalyn opens her mouth and smashes all of those preconceived thoughts with a single sentence.

"My first husband beat me for years before I was able to escape."

I listened with tears in my eyes as she spoke of being alienated from her entire family so the man who was supposed to love her could control and hurt her.

Then Misty spoke of her religious upbringing, of her parents' willingness to disown her, and how she sat at the clinic, mere moments away from aborting her first son Griffin before she realized she could have a different life.

Khloe spoke about losing her best friend in the Middle East, and how she downed a bottle of pills because she didn't see another way of moving on.

Then they talked about Diego, Morrison, and Dustin, the men of the Cerberus MC that arrived at just the right time to change everything for them, and I feel kindred with these women because that's exactly what happened for me with Ryan. And as the day goes on and the conversation continues, I allow myself to think of a future. By the time evening rolls around and the diamond painting has transformed from a sticky mess to a sparkling piece of art, I've forgiven myself.

I forgive myself for smiling at the stranger at the mall.

I forgive myself for not fighting harder when I was having really bad days at the compound.

I forgive myself for hurting, for staying in bed longer than I should have, for being afraid because what happened to me was terrible.

And when Emmalyn offers to let me stay in her guest bedroom so I won't be all alone in the clubhouse, I agree because there's safety in numbers and these women aren't different from me. The only thing that they have over me is time. They've had time to heal, time to accept that they deserve more than they were initially offered, time to love those that love them.

They deserve it.

And I deserve it, too.

Chapter 17

Scooter

I'm distracted more today than I have ever been.

I'm distracted by the scent of her on my t-shirt that I refused to change when I woke up.

I'm distracted by the warmth of her skin I swear I can still feel on my lips from when I pressed them to her forehead before crawling out of bed.

I'm distracted by the need to run back to her even though we've only been in South America for a handful of hours.

"You're distracted," Jinx says as he walks up to me.

I chuckle with his observation. It's like the man is in my head.

"Distraction is dangerous. Distractions will get you killed," he adds.

"I'll be fine."

"Distractions can get me killed," he continues, rubbing his hand along his scruffy jawline. "I'm too pretty to die, so you need to get your head in the fucking game and leave New Mexico and Mia behind until this mission is over."

"I'm fine," I snap.

When my phone chimes in my pocket, he raises an eyebrow when I reach for it.

"You're distracted," he repeats before walking away.

He isn't telling me anything I haven't already thought of myself but hearing concern for his own safety and anticipating that I'll be the cause if something goes wrong makes me take a step back and reevaluate.

The text is from Mia, the very first one she's sent me since I programmed my number into her cell before leaving. I'm turning my phone upside down, trying to figure out what in the hell the glittery thing is in the image when another text comes in.

Mia: I've been diamond painting with the girls today.

"Diamond painting?" I mutter.

"Em loves it."

I nearly drop my phone when Kincaid sneaks up on me.

I won't get into trouble for getting a text message, but I stow my phone back in my pocket because I don't want my boss to come to the same conclusion both Jinx and I have.

"Em also says that Mia stayed at our house all day while they worked on it, and she's agreed to stay the night there as well."

This news calms some of my fears. I was terrified she'd have a nightmare and there'd be no one there to comfort her, or worse, she'd end up leaving because I was gone.

"She's safe and from what Em said, she's happy right now." Kincaid slaps me on the back. "So, get your head in the game, so we can all make it back home safe, yeah?"

I nod and follow him to the huge table set up in the center of the main room of the command center.

More than forty men are grouped around waiting for final details and intel.

"Those the new guys?" I angle my head at the men I don't recognize.

It's not uncommon to have a few unfamiliar faces when we have a job to do. Shadow and Blade have always been adamant that we involve local forces as much as we can without compromising our main focus, but there's at least a dozen men in addition to the federal agents.

"Yeah," Rocker says. "That's only half the team. There are ten still back at the hotel."

"And Jinx was worried about me having his six. Can we trust hired guns?"

"Technically, we're the hired guns," Rocker mutters. "I've never worked with their entire team, but we did a job six years ago and a couple of these guys tagged along. They're like the Rambos of infiltration, recon, and recovery."

"You make them sound like they're better than we are." We both chuckle, our hard-earned egos not allowing us to let those thoughts sit very long.

"I saw one guy take a shotgun blast to the vest, and he didn't even flinch," Rocker adds, and I know he's thinking about taking the hits to the chest in Miami that laid him out for a couple days. "They're in this for the money, but they're efficient as hell. I'm glad they're here."

"If you trust them; I'll trust them."

He nods at me, and his faith in them is all I need to have the same.

"This is going to go a little faster than we initially thought," Kincaid says from the head of the table.

All the guys turn to statues. We're in the window of time where all jokes, all thoughts of everything else going on in our lives have to fall to the wayside. Errors at this point can lead to death, and that's unacceptable.

"As much as we tried to prevent it, Cortez and Jiménez know that we're here. Although we hoped we could sneak in undetected, it's difficult to move sixty men into a country without drawing some attention," Kincaid continues.

Sixty men? That's one hell of a platoon. In the Marine Corps, we took over small towns in Turkey with a lot fewer men. My confidence grows as Kincaid talks about what we're facing.

"They're ready for us. They're armed to the teeth, but so are we." We all look down at the aerial maps spread out on the table as Kincaid points out areas of focus. "Twelve men from Blackbridge Security will go to Luis Cortez's compound. Movement around there has been minimal the last three days. All of Cerberus and the remaining men from Blackbridge will infiltrate Xavier Cortez's compound."

"With the way they've set up their defenses," Shadow begins as he points to the property in front of Xavier's compound, "they're expecting us to enter here. Team C will be bottlenecked in this area. We expect heavy fire since intel has revealed this is where they expect us to hit the hardest."

Shadow has that glint in his eyes that I have grown to love so much. The thrill of the fight begins to seep into my veins, and all other thoughts slip away.

"The National Bolivarian Armed Forces reluctantly provided us with a few toys to ensure we're able to breech the property here." Shadow indicates the area at the back of the compound as far away from the front entrance as possible.

"Toys?" Jinx asks.

"Nothing major," Shadow says with a smirk. "A couple tanks and a few rocket launchers."

Several of us around the table chuckle, and Kincaid waits until it dies down before he picks back up.

The final details are laid out. Each team is given their micro orders, but one question grows in my mind, and from the looks on the other guys' faces, I know they're thinking it, too.

"Any questions?" Kincaid asks after the tank drivers ask about specifics on structural things so the compound doesn't come down around us.

Several of us look around, but I finally take a step forward and speak up, "What's the order on prisoners?"

Kincaid looks to Shadow and his brother Dominic before making eye contact with Deacon Black, the founder of Blackbridge Security.

"Take none," he finally says when his eyes make it back to mine.

"That being said," Dominic interrupts after a loud whoop and cheers from the other men dies down. "It's our duty to protect the women they're holding hostage. We have a rough count of over twenty inside. If we're lucky, they'll all be grouped together, but we know how quick luck runs out with these guys. So be careful, and when in doubt let God sort 'em out."

We all nod because that's always understood. No matter what, we go home. That's always the rule.

"And Gabrielle Butler?" Jinx asks.

"The CIA would like to interrogate her, but at the end of the day she's considered turned and is with Jiménez now. If she pulls on you, take her down." Kincaid says the words like they don't affect him, but I know he doesn't take giving the kill order of a woman lightly.

We're infiltrating at three in the morning, so we're ushered out of the command center to a small ranch that the federal government recently commandeered under the orders of getting some rest.

With any luck, we'll be back home in New Mexico in less than twenty-four hours.

Chapter 18

Mia

I'm startled more than I should be when my ringing phone jolts me from sleep. It hasn't rung once since I got it.

My pulse spikes when the sound continues, but it has nothing on the way I feel when I see Ryan's club name 'Scooter' on the screen.

"H-hello," I mumble, my voice not working well since I was sleeping.

"It's late. I shouldn't have called."

"No, it's fine," I insist as I sit up on the bed and pull the covers up to my chin.

"You were sleeping. I know how hard that is for you when…" He clears his throat. "I'm sorry I woke you up."

I know what he was going to say, and he's right. It is harder for me to sleep when he's not here, but I wore myself out today. I didn't do much physically but hanging out with the girls without my normal nap left me exhausted and ready for bed.

"I'm at Emmalyn's," I tell him.

"Kincaid told me you were staying there. I'm glad you spent some time with them today."

It's implied that he's glad I didn't stay holed up in the room all day.

"It's so quiet here with everyone gone."

I want to tell him I miss him, that I want him to come home soon. I want to let him know that I feel safe, but I'd feel better if he were lying beside me with his arms wrapped around my body. I shiver, a quick tremble working over my entire body in his absence.

"Is it too quiet?" I hear a rustling sound, and I wonder if he's in bed, too. "I don't want you getting stuck in your head."

"The girls didn't allow for it today. I don't know what tomorrow brings, though."

"Don't." He sighs, the gust of his breath filling my ear. "Stay positive. I'll be home soon."

"How soon?"

"I can't—I don't know. That's not something I can discuss."

"I understand."

I do, sort of. I'm aware of what he does in the grand scheme of things. I was one of his rescues after all. I know he's in Venezuela, and they plan to take down the men that hurt me and countless other women in Miami. I can picture what that looks like. The gunfire before he opened the door that day still echoes in my nightmares.

"I wish I was there with you."

His soft confession makes me smile, and I bite the inside of my cheek to hide it as if he can see me right now.

"I'm sharing a room with Jinx, and he snores like a freight train. At least you don't snore."

I refuse to remind him that I whimper a lot in my sleep. I know I do because it wakes me up, thankfully most nights before the nightmares can claw their way inside of me.

"Emmalyn's guest room is lovely." I roll my lips, unsure if I want to add the second part, but I figure his confession and the soft kiss we shared before he left is enough to make me spill my guts as well. "It would be better if you were under the covers with me."

Silence fills the line, and I wonder if I've gone too far, said more than he wants to hear.

A groan breaks the silence, and it's gravelly enough to make me quiver, the sound settling low in my gut, making me feel things I thought I'd never feel for as long as I live. It's only a hint, but I recognize my own arousal.

And then the shame hits me.

After what happened to me, I shouldn't feel this way. I shouldn't want him here with his hands on my skin and his lips at my throat. I shouldn't be able to imagine myself sharing any form of intimacy with a man.

"I'm sorry," I apologize. "I shouldn't have said that."

I shouldn't be feeling this. That thought echoes in my head, and shame makes me pull the covers closer around me until I'm cocooned in the blanket. The soft scent of fabric softener fills my nose, but it brings me no comfort.

I'm debating whether or not to hang up, praying that when he returns, he won't look at me differently when I hear him shift again on his end of the line.

"I'd give almost anything to be there with you. It's what I want, too." He sighs again, and I don't know if he's frustrated with the physical distance between us or if he's agitated that he said something he feels he shouldn't have said.

"I put you on the spot. I didn't mean to make things uncomfortable."

"You know what I would do if I were there right now?" His husky voice, and the thoughts running through my head make another rush of goosebumps cover my skin. "I would cup your face with both of my hands."

I can feel his skin on mine even from hundreds of miles away. I let my eyes flutter closed so I can picture exactly what he's describing.

"You'll want to look away from me, of that I'm certain, but I won't let you. I'm a patient man, Mia, and I'll stand there for days if I have to, just taking in your beautiful face until your eyes meet mine."

I inhale a ragged breath, because I know he would. He's more patient than any other person I've ever met.

"And when you do, Sweet Mia, I'll remind you how perfect you are. I'll remind you that you're the most beautiful woman I've ever laid eyes on. I'll ask you to see in yourself what I see in you every second of every day. That you're not what happened to you, that it doesn't define who you are going forward, and when you're ready, you'll overcome all of it, becoming someone stronger in the end. And I want to be there every step of the way. I want to celebrate your victories and hold you when you're not strong enough to stand on your own two feet."

Tears leak from my closed eyes, leaving a trail of wetness down my face.

"So in short, you aren't making things uncomfortable for me. You haven't a single time since we met. You're not putting me on the spot with your confessions. You're giving me hope that one day I can tell you everything. One day I can confess the things you're not ready to hear just yet. So say whatever is on your mind. Don't hide things from me. Don't sugarcoat your feelings. If you're happy, tell me. If you're missing me, tell me. If I rub you the wrong way or piss you off, tell me that, too. I want to hear it all."

"Where did you come from?" I whisper.

Is he actually perfect, or is he so different from the men that hurt me that I'm putting him on some sort of pedestal?

"Nebraska originally, but we moved around a lot when I was younger."

A laugh escapes my throat, and it makes him chuckle, too. I already knew he was born there. He disclosed that information during the time he was regaling me with stories of his childhood.

I'm torn between whispering the same stories of growing up and keeping my past exactly where it is, behind me.

Not everything was terrible growing up. Honestly, until we got word that Max had died in a car accident, things were pretty awesome. That was before Jason, before the abduction, before the weeks and weeks of pain and degradation.

"Will you kill them all?" I ask, instead of beginning my own trip down memory lane.

It says a lot of how much I want to avoid that topic considering the question I just asked.

"I don't know."

He doesn't sigh this time. He doesn't sound annoyed that I asked him about his work. I know he can't say much, but I trust that he will tell me as much as he can.

"Do you want to kill them all?"

"Every last fucking one of them," he says without pausing to think about it.

"I want that, too," I confess. "Does that make me a vengeful bitch?"

"Not even close to one."

"If you get the chance, kill them all."

I wonder what that would do for his psyche. I wonder if pulling the trigger and snuffing out the life of another human being keeps him up at night. If he regrets the things he's done to save women like me.

Even after what I've been through, I don't know if I have what it takes to kill even the vilest men that hurt me personally, and I know it's asking a lot to have someone else do that on my behalf. Most of those men met their maker in Miami, but I know Luis Jiménez somehow managed to escape. I pray he doesn't make it out alive this time around.

"You have my word," he vows.

"There are women involved also," I tell him.

I'm still drained from the conversation we had last night, but he needs to know that it's not only men capable of doing horrible things.

He does exactly what he did last night, keeping quiet and letting me speak rather than asking a ton of questions. He saw how I reacted in the hospital when the federal agents came to get my statement. They didn't get anything out of me, and I think he fears the same.

"Gabi was already there when I arrived, but one of the girls said she was abducted just like the rest of us. Some of the girls pretended to like what the guys were doing to them, but at night they still cried themselves to sleep, still tried to hurt themselves to make it all end. Gabi was different. She somehow convinced the guys that she was exactly where she wanted to be. She helped—" a sob wracks my body, interrupting my words, and I hate myself for how weak I still am.

"Sweet Mia," Ryan says through the phone. "God, I wish I was there to hold you. You don't have to put yourself through this."

But I do. I woke up this morning feeling more human than I have in a long time, and I'm sure it had a lot to do with getting some of this stuff off my chest.

"She helped them hurt us. It's like she got off on torturing women. She'd hold us down, help tie us up, hit us with her fists or any object she could get her hands on. She's an awful person." I sniffle. "I wanted you to know in case she made it out of Miami. She's not a victim. Or at least she wasn't by the time you guys came into the compound. She was the one who killed Sara. Sara was hiding some sort of secret about Gabi and threatened to tell one of the guards, and Gabi didn't blink when she bashed her head in."

An eerie calm settles over me, the numbness reminiscent of how I was beginning to feel back at the compound. It makes me feel less than human, and I hate it.

"Anyone else we need to know about?" He doesn't grill me any further.

"They didn't let me out of the room very often," I inform him. "I was trouble, fighting them constantly. They had visitors all the time."

"Visitors?"

One simple word in the form of a question. I could easily shut down the conversation right now, but I want to help them as much as I can. It could be information they need to prevent this from happening to someone else.

"The girls that were good at pretending were allowed out during their parties. Unless one of their guests asked about a girl with fight still left in her, I stayed locked away. I know an MC club visited not long ago. Raven something or other."

"They hurt you?" The growl of his voice is low and threatening.

"No. I didn't leave the room that night. The only reason the girls thought it was weird was because the president and vice president wouldn't touch any of them. Luis wasn't impressed by that at all. He doesn't like it when people show up and don't sample what he's offering."

The blanket around me is no longer enough. Somehow the cold seeps inside of me, and I miss Ryan even more desperately.

He must sense the change because he drops the subject.

"What are you wearing?"

A chuckle escapes my throat, and if he were anyone else, I'd go postal on him for asking such a question after the things I just told him about, but Ryan isn't just anyone. He's the man that's been there for the darkest times of my life.

"I'm naked," I tease, biting my lip and praying this conversation doesn't get out of hand.

"Liar," he huffs. "I know better than that."

"I'm wearing your blue t-shirt and a pair of black leggings. I had your hoodie on, but it got to hot once I was in bed. I also have on a pair of fuzzy socks that were in the bag that Jasmine brought over. What are you wearing?"

He clears his throat, and for a second, I think he's going to lie to me. "Boxers."

"Only boxers?"

"We don't exactly pack for luxury when we work."

"What color are they?"

He groans, and I hear the rustle of his sheets.

"Black."

"Of course they are." Ryan doesn't have much color in his wardrobe. Honestly, from what I've seen of the other guys, none of them wear much other than black and gray.

I yawn, and it comes on so fast, I'm unable to pull the phone away from my mouth.

"You need to get some rest."

"I'm not tired," I lie, but I know he won't believe it, so I slide down in the bed, turning to my side and tugging the pillow I was holding in his absence closer.

"We're heading out in just a little while," he says. "I'll call you when I can. Sleep well, Sweet Mia."

We hang up, and once again the room fills with a deafening silence.

I'm unable to go back to sleep, my mind opting to worry about him instead.

Chapter 19

Scooter

"Gabriella Butler is definitely on Jiménez's side," I tell Kincaid the first time I see him mere hours after I got off the phone with Mia. "She helped torture the women there. Mia says she's the one who killed Agent Sara DeMoss."

Kincaid nods, and I know he's still trying to wrap his head around women hurting other women and enjoying it, but this is a cruel fucking world, and it's ignorant to think that only testosterone-riddled men are capable of gruesome things.

The next hour is spent gearing up in fatigues, strapping on weapons, and checking and then double-checking that we have everything we'll need.

Thankfully, I'm able to find a quiet corner so I can get my head straight. That means blocking out the sound of Mia's voice in my head, the scent of her skin, which I still swear I can smell when I breathe deeply.

Kill them all.

Although I try to clear my mind of everything else, her words echo in my head, becoming my mantra for the day. I couldn't tell her that we were given that order. People would be in an uproar if they knew that on many occasions, we're told to leave no one standing. Human life is valuable. That's proven by the saturation of sex trafficking around the world. It's a market reliant on the abduction, rape, and torture of men, women, and children, and it's become an epidemic, a virus touching the lives of too many people.

We end some of that today. In less than an hour, we'll rid the world of three major players in the South American sex trade. I won't even let myself consider a different outcome. The Cortez brothers and Jiménez will not see the sun rise ever again. Even if I have to make sacrifices that prevent me from returning to New Mexico, I'll have their blood on my boots before the sky transitions from night to day.

"Ready?" Kincaid asks from the head of the table in the command post.

We all nod as echoes of magazines being slid into place make their way around the room.

We split into five teams as we walk out of the building. Four are heading to the main compound, and one team, made up solely of Blackbridge men, is heading to the smaller one.

The men manning the two tanks are already in position. I'm on Bravo Team with Jinx, Hound, and Snatch. As we drive to our drop point, my leg bounces with adrenaline and hatred for these types of men.

Jinx leans in close, his shoulder still a few inches from mine due to all the gear we're wearing. We aren't any more heavily armed than we normally are. We enter each raid as if we're traversing Hell, and we're prepared for anything.

"Is your head where it needs to be?" I nod, because it is. My few moments of meditation earlier compartmentalized the parts of Mia that have no business with me right now, and my only focus is clearing this compound. "You seem anxious."

"I'm great," I tell him, and deep in my bones I know it's the truth.

Maybe things being personal is a good thing. It makes me want the victory that much more.

We don't have time for more conversation because the armored vehicle we're riding in jolts to a stop and we pile out of the back.

"Keep ten feet behind the tank," Snatch says as we exit. "They're going to break through the concrete wall and open up a pathway. Each of you know your assignments. Be safe. Kill them all."

That's as good as instructions from God himself as far as I'm concerned. I don't imagine getting stuck on the wrong side of the pearly gates because I put a bullet in some asshole's head is going to happen, and if it does... worth it.

With a clear head and my focus where it should be, I don't even jerk when an explosion is heard from the other side of the property.

"That's our cue," Snatch says into his mic. "Alpha Team has made their presence known at the front gates."

With this news, the tank starts to roll forward, moving much quicker than one would expect from a twenty-six-ton vehicle.

We keep our distance as the distant firefight continues.

Stupidly, Cortez never imagined that someone would have the ability to breach his property from the back because the house is only thirty yards from the property line, and in a matter of minutes we're using the battering ram on the back door.

Bullets fly from the top of the compound, but the tank raises its main gun and blasts a hole the size of an SUV. Our Kevlar helmets protect our heads from falling debris, and on the third slam of the battering ram on the door, it swings open. We're met with a hail of bullets, but a couple of flash bangs shuts that shit down quickly.

We move in with the smoke, my own weapon firing at anything that moves, planting bullets in soft flesh until all movement stops. Strategically, according to the plans that were drilled into our heads at the command center, we move from room to room. They have more men than we do, but they aren't nearly as prepared or experienced as we are.

"They're all dead," Grinch hisses into his mic.

"We haven't even made it to the second floor," Shadow responds. "There's still more to neutralize."

"The women," Grinch specifies. "The basement is filled with the dead bodies. They killed all the women before we got here."

Rage fills my blood, but at the same time I'm also hit with a sense of relief that this happened here and not in Miami. I couldn't imagine what my life would be like without Mia in it.

"Stay focused," Kincaid says. "We still have a job to do."

I swallow the lump of emotion that is trying to form in my throat and move across the floor as planned. There isn't a thing we can do for those women now except making every one of these fuckers pay with their lives.

Two more men drop in front of me, the triple burst of my weapon making it easy, and my feet shuffle me deeper inside. The acrid scent of gunpowder seeps into my system, and I remember why I love this job so much. These men dropping in front of me mean absolutely nothing. I don't feel a thing other than unadulterated joy to watch them crumple to the ground at my feet, but I'm not here for the hired guns. I want the three men running this ship.

Since we didn't have enough intel to know where they'd be in the house, they couldn't be targeted by any specific team, but I'm making it my personal mission to watch the light fade from Jiménez's eyes, and a bonus for that deviant bitch he's taken under his wing. The CIA won't learn any more than they already know about her and letting her walk out of this compound still breathing the South American air isn't an option.

Like the tactical team we are, the first floor is cleared. Twelve men, six on each, split between the two staircases, each of us popping off rounds as targets present themselves. Part of the ceiling collapsed from the tank fire, but we manage to work our way around it easily enough.

The second floor is cleared in a matter of minutes, and still no one has confirmed the elimination of any of the three main targets.

"Blackbridge confirms that Luis Cortez was neutralized across town," Shadow says into his mic.

That's one down, I think as I clear the closet in an extravagant bedroom. Personal items are on the dresser, including an expensive looking set of cufflinks, and there's a discarded pair of high heels near the bed. This room is too nice for guests, so our targets can't be far.

"Jinx, I need thermal in here."

He was mere feet behind me when I entered the room, so it doesn't take long until he's by my side. Jinx scans the room, and he doesn't find anything until a halo of color appears on his screen around the huge painting in the walk-in closet.

"Xavier Cortez is down," Kincaid announces. "Panic room in the closet. It took an ounce of plastic to get to him."

"Jiménez has to be in there," Jinx says as he walks toward the painting.

I cover his back as he rips the priceless piece of shit from the wall.

Sure enough, there's a door that has a keypad lock on it. In a matter of seconds, it's rigged with the explosive, and Jinx and I take cover on the outside of the closet for detonation.

Smoke fills the closet, but it's no more than what we're used to. Jinx covers me while I swing the door open. We wait for a break in the gunfire before engaging.

Cursing and a woman sobbing can be heard, and then I realize that Jiménez and Gabriella Butler are in here alone. This fool thought a steel door controlled by an electric panel was going to be enough to keep him and his whore safe? Ignorant. He doesn't have men guarding him or have an anteroom for added protection. Butler is cowering at his side while he tries to figure out why his weapon misfired. He's spouting curse words in Spanish at such a rate it sounds like one long insult.

Without a word, I put three bullets in Butler. She doesn't even have time to protest before she's gone. I'm glad that Mia didn't give me specifics about how Gabi helped the men hurt her. They wouldn't even be able to identify the damn body if she had.

Jiménez wails as he's racked with genuine sorrow. He jostles Butler's body, pulling her to his lap, and it's clear that he's just lost the love of his life. He doesn't have to worry though, before long he'll be joining her in Hell.

"You fucked up," I taunt him.

He rocks back and forth, begging in his native tongue for none of this to be true.

Jinx reloads beside me, but I hold my hand up to keep him from ending this before I have the chance to do it myself. The order was to kill them all, but my desire to string him up and torture him for days or weeks or months is stronger than I ever anticipated.

I can already hear the conversation about ethics coming from Shadow and Kincaid, so I know I'll only have a few minutes before I spray him with bullets.

"Your days of hurting people is over," I tell him, but I don't think he can hear me over his own sobs.

Not having his undivided attention annoys me so I unholster my Glock from my hip and shoot him in the leg, down low on his shin to avoid him bleeding out too quickly.

Jiménez yelps in pain, forgetting his dead woman as he grabs for the new injury.

"I fucking hate men like you." I crouch low and look him in the eye.

"Scooter," Jinx warns.

None of this is protocol. Protocol would've been shooting him without hurting the woman the second we entered the room. Right now, I'm a predator playing with the prey, and that's frowned upon with Cerberus. Hell, it's grounds for being released from my contract with the club, but in this moment, I'm fine with that outcome.

"You see—"

Funny that I'm saying those words when I don't actually see Jiménez pull a pistol from his boot. This gun doesn't backfire like his first one did. He gets off at least three rounds, screaming like a vigilantly before Jinx lights his ass up. His body shakes and jerks like he's being electrocuted, each bullet hitting center mass.

I feel like I've been hit by the tank outside and runover twice as I lose my balance and crash backward. All I can remember is the chipped paint on the concrete ceiling before my world begins to fade. My last thought before the darkness takes over is that I knew a sacrifice had to be made today, and all three men are dead. It's what Mia needs to start healing.

Chapter 20

Mia

My mind is racing.

He promised he'd call.

He hasn't.

Not wanting to interrupt his work since I know how dangerous it is, I haven't tried calling or texting him either.

He said they were going to raid the compounds shortly after we got off the phone. That was twelve hours ago, and I've yet to hear a peep.

With my phone in my hand, I make my way downstairs. It's early evening, and dinner was tense with the girls. There wasn't much conversation, and I could easily tell that they were just as worried as I was, which concerned me even more because as the wives of these guys, they've been doing this for years and years.

Emmalyn smiles at me as I enter the living room. She's on the sofa with a book in her hands. The tension from earlier seems to be gone.

"Have you heard from Diego?"

She frowns at me, and I'm terrified she's going to give me horrible news, but my phone rings in my hand.

'Scooter' flashes on the screen, and I don't even bother saying a word to Emmalyn before turning around and flying back up the stairs to the room I stayed in last night.

"Hello?" My voice cracks when I answer, but I'm still too worried to care.

"Sweet Mia," Ryan breathes into the phone.

Relief washes over me instantly, but it doesn't stop the tremble in my hands.

"I thought you'd call sooner," I complain, feeling like an old mother hen.

He chuckles, but even through the phone, I can tell there's no humor in his voice.

"I've been worried about you."

"I'm fine. Everyone is okay."

He's called like he promised, but it's clear he doesn't really want to talk.

"How did it go?" I ask, needing to keep him on the line. His voice is the only thing that's keeping me sane.

"I can't really talk about the mission." He sighs loudly, and it's the most frustrating sound.

"Are they dead? Is *he* dead?"

I know they were going after three men, but he knows which one I'm asking about specifically. Luis Jiménez haunts my every thought.

"He's dead," he confirms. "They're all dead."

It feels like a ten-ton weight has been lifted from my shoulders. In an instant I feel lighter, knowing those evil men will no longer walk the earth. They will no longer hurt people. Knowing that their final breaths have been taken alleviates some of the shame and brokenness that's been tormenting me.

"Thank you," I whisper.

He can't possibly know what his actions mean for my mental well-being.

Or maybe he does. Maybe he can sense the change I already feel deep inside of myself. I want him here. I need to see that he's okay. I want to wrap my arms around him, brush my lips against his. I want to hold him against me and beg him to never go away again.

"Anything for you, Sweet Mia."

"When will you be back?"

Silence fills the line, and I can't help but feel like he's hiding something. Everything isn't okay. There's something wrong and he's keeping it to himself. I hate the distance between us right now, both physically and emotionally, but I can't blame him. I've been distant myself for weeks. I've only given him peeks at who I am now, afraid opening up to him fully will only lead to more pain and anger.

"I don't know," he finally answers. "We have a lot of shit left to do."

"Is there more danger?" I'm a fool for thinking it's over. It's never over. It'll never be over. Just because those three evil men are gone doesn't mean a damn thing. There're other men. Men ready to take their places. Men already operating in a world where women serve no purpose other than being toys meant to be played with and defiled. Cerberus will never be able to rid the world of those men. They're fighting a losing battle, one that grows exponentially every day.

"There's always more danger," he confirms. "Always another piece of shit. Always another compound to raid. Always another woman to rescue."

I snap my mouth shut, hating that he seems to be able to read my mind. It's also worrisome that he's telling me these things now when normally he'd keep these truths to himself. Something has shifted. Something is different, and I hate it. I don't necessarily want to be lied to or placated, but it's out of character for him to speak these truths to me, especially when it doesn't come with his normal assurances that he'll continue to keep me safe or telling me that they're doing their best and will continue to fight the monsters most people only hear about on the evening news.

"Listen, Mia. I have to go."

He hangs up before I can tell him bye or drill him for more answers. The silence coming through on my cell phone is deafening, yet I hold the thing to my ear with the hope that I'm mistaken. He didn't just shut me down with a few whispered words.

Tears burn my eyes, and even though I vowed my crying days were over, I do nothing to stop them from spilling down my face.

My nose stings, causing me to sniffle, and I hate myself for not being able to find the strength I was sure I was building since I came to New Mexico. I feel weak once again. I feel needy and lost.

Is this what he's like after every mission? Maybe he needs some time to process what he's done.

Does killing those men weigh on him like I expected before? I don't imagine it's easy to pull a trigger and end a life, no matter how heinous the people were.

I stiffen my back, keeping my eyes focused on the window until my tears dry. He said he was okay, and I have to believe that he is. He called, so that means physically he's fine, but I also know that it's the mental pains and injuries that take the longest to heal.

I vow to be what he needs when he gets home, just like he was for me. We can heal together. I can be everything that he needs and more.

If he's willing to let me.

A knock on the bedroom door jolts me from my thoughts, and I give Emmalyn a weak smile when she sticks her head inside.

"Did Scooter call?"

I nod, smiling when I hear his club name. I only think of him as Ryan, but everyone else calls him Scooter. Maybe I enjoy it so much because I know that they are two different people. Ryan is the one who holds me at night when the nightmares keep me from wanting to close my eyes. He's the one who crawled into the hospital bed with me when I couldn't find peace. He's the one that protects me while still being able to let me gain some of my own independence.

Scooter goes after the bad guys. He rids the world of trash and evil men.

Now I'm wondering if I just spoke to Scooter, instead of Ryan. Maybe that's the difference. Maybe since he's away and working he doesn't have the ability to be the man I know. Maybe he's only capable of being Scooter right now.

That thought calms me even further because I know the man that will come back will be the man I need, just like I'll be the woman he needs.

"They're all safe," Emmalyn says when I don't respond further. "That's all we ever ask for. Now come downstairs and join us for dinner and a movie. We only have another day or so until the guys come back and make so much noise, we think we're going crazy."

I don't even hesitate to climb off the bed and follow her to the living room. When I see that she has delivery pizza on the table along with individual salads, I feel a rush of guilt. I've been using these people every day since I arrived. I haven't pulled my weight or helped out in any capacity. I hate using people, so I make another vow, one that includes helping and doing what I can to make things around here easier for everyone.

"I hope you like veggies," Misty says as she pours a couple glasses of wine. "When the guys get home, all they want is meat and more meat on their pizzas."

I cup my hand over the glass in front of my place setting, letting her know I don't want wine, and she lets me know that there's soda and bottled water in the fridge.

She doesn't frown or try to convince me that a little alcohol wouldn't hurt me, and I'm grateful to have found these amazing women.

We settle in with our food and drinks and watch three romantic comedies before the night is over.

And we're all counting down the minutes until the guys come home. Knowing they're okay and seeing it with our own eyes are two different things.

Chapter 21
Scooter

"Fuck," I grunt after hanging up on Mia.

I already feel like a piece of shit for what went down in Jimenez's panic room. Now I'm an even bigger asshole for hanging up on my girl.

I huff a humorless laugh. *My girl.* What a damn joke.

Mia doesn't belong to anyone. She doesn't want to be owned. She experienced that for weeks, and even though I'd never hurt her like those bastards did, I'm fairly certain it's not something she'd even entertain. No matter how many times she brushes her lips across mine or how many times she holds me in her sleep.

She'll never be mine.

And I'm a fool for even holding out hope.

I scrape rough hands over the top of my head, trying to rid it of all thoughts of her. She's the cause for today, but she's not to blame for my actions, rather my inability to separate things is the reason. This is all on me, and even though the bullets have stopped flying, I'm not even close to being done dealing with this shit.

I sense Kincaid drawing closer before he even says a word. I don't know how bad the fallout is going to be, but I know I won't be able to walk away from what happened today without some sort of discipline.

"Ryan," Kincaid says as he steps up beside me.

Shit is bad, really bad if he's using my legal name rather than my club name. It's a way to remind me that I'm an employee long before I'm a friend.

"Sir," I answer, standing tall and praying he doesn't see it as a defensive act.

There's no way for me to defend what I did, and I hope he's aware that I know it.

"May I speak with you alone?" He angles his head to the side, indicating an empty room.

We're still in the compound, working on cleanup. There are more bodies here than we've ever had on a mission before, including the women that were slaughtered in the basement.

I follow him without a word, and the closing door echoes around us, ringing like we're being enclosed in a tomb.

Instinctively, I want to apologize before he even opens his mouth, but I can't manage the words. I don't know that I am sorry for taunting

Jiménez. I'm only sorry that I wasn't paying enough attention and nearly got myself killed. I'm sorry that Jinx gets to claim that kill because I was careless. As if thinking about it activates the pain, the impact wounds on my chest burn like fire. I'm going to be sore for days.

"You're normally so focused," Kincaid begins. "What you did today was not only against Cerberus protocol, but it was foolish. You endangered your life and the life of a teammate."

I swallow thickly, unable to argue a single point because he's right.

"If you're given a kill order, it's what you do. Find, aim, shoot. It's that simple. Taunting a mark is not only unprofessional, going against everything that Cerberus stands for, but it's dangerous. Normally you take your job very seriously. You're not one of the guys I have to worry about. You're a machine on missions, and you take down the targets and move on to the next."

I've disappointed him, and that concerns me more than endangering my life. I feel like shit for putting Jinx in the middle of it. My throat burns with letting him down. He's my boss, but he's also a mentor, a father-like figure that I respect without fail.

"I was distracted," I tell him, and we both know that it's only part of it.

"The entire team and the men from Blackbridge heard you taunting Jiménez. Everyone knows you took Butler out without following protocol. She was to be interrogated by the CIA."

I stiffen further, wondering what this means for my career with Cerberus. Hell, killing her could bring formal criminal charges. There's a possibility I'll end up in prison for what happened today.

"It's Mia, isn't it?" My head snaps in his direction, but I don't find irritation on his face. "I understand, believe me. We all have people back home that we love, people we worry about when we're working, but you can't let them control your actions and your thoughts. We won't make it home to them, your team won't make it home to the people they care about if you can't get that under control."

"I don't know how to do that. I'm beyond distracted. I was livid walking into that panic room," I confess. "I wanted to take him apart piece by piece. I wanted to bathe in his fucking blood."

Kincaid nods, and I can tell he fully understands what I'm feeling. The only difference is, Kincaid was able to kill the man who hurt Emmalyn when he had the balls to go to the clubhouse to take her back. I fucked up so royally that Jinx had to do my dirty work.

"I understand exactly how you feel, believe me, but the kill order should've been enough. It has to be enough. Even if he was unarmed and you had all the time in the world, a bullet in the head is all you can do. We're not those men. We're not allowed to get off on torturing them. We're moral men. We're a moral club, and you have to decide if you're able to operate under those orders."

"I couldn't separate her out. I could only see red where he was concerned."

"You have to compartmentalize. You have to box her away while you're working. Every man that we go after is like Jiménez. Every one of them hurt women. Everyone could easily have been the one to hurt Mia or Emmalyn but making it personal makes it dangerous."

"Yes, sir," I tell him, even though I know how hard it'll be to just work now without making things personal. Before Mia, I operated like a robot. I had my mission, and I always executed it with precision and efficiency. Things are different now. Now, I'm exorcising her demons, the demons of all the women ever hurt, and that changes things drastically. I can no longer operate without emotion. It's impossible. The only thing left is to figure out if I can box them away like he suggests.

"You're suspended for a month, longer if the CIA is still investigating. When we return to New Mexico, you'll undergo psych testing to determine when and if you're able to return to fieldwork."

"Yes, sir."

Suddenly, his demeanor changes, and he steps closer, cupping my shoulder with his palm. "Loving someone and being able to handle this job will be one of the hardest things you'll ever have to do. I have faith that you can do it, but if you can't, there's no harm in that either."

He walks away, leaving me in the quiet room questioning my entire future.

What would I have if I didn't have Cerberus?

Would Mia even want to stick around when I could no longer protect her with the backing of the club?

I have a million thoughts racing through my head when I leave the room to continue with cleanup. The deceased women are treated with more respect than the men who hurt them as we enclose each one into a body bag. Some we're able to identify, like Caroline Spring, the woman we didn't find from our last mission in Venezuela. The woman abducted from a mission trip weeks and weeks ago was crouched over, clearly protecting two younger girls. Her tiny body didn't protect her or them from the spray of bullets.

Thankfully, the Blackbridge men stay out of the basement. They're upstairs sifting through paperwork after we identified the body of the woman who was abducted while under the protection of Deacon Black's men.

The CIA is working on identifying all the men we dropped during the raid and updating their databases in preparation for retaliation from those men's family members. There's always a little fallout when working a mission. It's why the women at the clubhouse are so well trained and protected.

Jinx works beside me, but he won't even look at me. I've damaged that relationship with him, and probably the relationship with all the other guys, since they were able to hear me taunting Jiménez.

I embarrassed all the men of Cerberus by my actions, and I did it in front of Blackbridge as well as the CIA. I can't imagine what all of them are thinking about me.

I won't make excuses for my behavior, but other than disappointing everyone, I don't regret it. My only regret is I let my guard down and Jinx had to end that fucker before I got to cut him up into tiny pieces. I'll regret as long as I live that I wasn't able to torture him until he begged me to let him die.

I was hoping to grow numb with each woman that I zip up in the generic black bags, but my anger only grows. I want to go back upstairs and kill all those fuckers all over again. The mass killing of these women and girls was pointless. All it did was serve as one last power play from men who knew they were going to die.

If this had happened in Miami, Max would've lost his twin sister, and I never would've met the woman who has the ability to change my entire life, and I feel like the worst person on earth for being grateful that it happened here instead of there.

Chapter 22

Mia

Electricity fills my blood while watching the guys pile out of the SUVs that rolled onto the property just a few seconds ago.

Misty, Khloe, and Emmalyn finish up the last touches to the meal we spent the morning preparing.

I haven't heard from Ryan since the phone call a couple of days ago, but that isn't stopping me from itching with adrenaline.

I notice Ryan right away, but the sour look on his face as I watch him grab his duffel out of the back of one SUV isn't what I'm expecting. I'm humming with a need to see him, to touch him, and to kiss him, and he looks like he's walking toward the gallows as he climbs the front steps to the clubhouse.

I don't know if it's all the men filtering through the front door that ups my anxiety, or the fact that Ryan isn't happy to be home.

I keep to the corner of the room, wondering if his face will change when he sees me, but I don't have to wait long. As if he can sense me in the room, his eyes dart to mine the second he's through the front door. I freeze, my heart pounding so hard, I'm sure it's going to bounce right out of my chest.

He doesn't drop his bag and run to me like I pictured would happen. He doesn't close the distance between the two of us like I see Diego do with Emmalyn and Dustin do with Khloe. He doesn't even shake my hand like Shadow does when his son Cannon walks up to him.

He doesn't walk toward me at all. He heads in the opposite direction, grabbing a beer from the fridge before turning to speak with one of the other guys.

It only takes a minute for me to realize I'm not wanted or not important enough. It angers me, pisses me off beyond belief, but calling him out on it isn't something I'd ever do in public, even if I wasn't shaking from being in a room with so many men.

While he's got his back turned, I disappear down the hallway, stopping outside my room before deciding to go to his. I'd never be able to sleep if I don't find out what his problem is. I need to know what's bothering him or if there's something I've done wrong.

So, I go to his room and sit in the dark. I'll wait here all night long if I have to. Ignoring problems and hoping they disappear isn't something I'm going to do to myself. I did that with Jason and the stress caused ulcers. I refuse to put myself in a similar situation. If he doesn't want me around, then he's going to have to use those words. We're both too damn old to let things fall apart because we can't communicate like adults.

Minutes turn into hours as I wait. The rambunctious crowd begins to dwindle, and yet Ryan is still absent. I'm nodding off in the center of his bed, still fully dressed when he finally shows his face. I know he can see me in here when he opens the door, but he doesn't bother with the light as he closes the door behind him.

His duffel thuds as he drops it to the floor, and a second later he's pulling his t-shirt over his head. Maybe he doesn't know I'm in here. Is he drunk? Even the thought doesn't bother me. Ryan wouldn't hurt me no matter what state he's in.

I click on the bedside lamp, but he doesn't even flinch as the bright light fills the room.

I gasp, however, because there are three huge bruises marring his otherwise perfect skin. The injuries are darker than the ink decorating his body.

"What happened?" I ask as I fly off the bed and reach for him.

He doesn't say a word as my fingers trace over the purple spots. He's frozen, a statue in the middle of his own room, and suddenly I feel like an intruder, unwelcome in a space I've always been welcomed before.

Yet, I'm stubborn, and if he wants me gone, he's going to have be a grown-up and use the words.

He doesn't open his mouth.

Not when I leave him standing to go get some cream from the bathroom.

Not when I apply the cold cream to his heated flesh.

Not when I brush my lips across his back while checking for more spots to doctor.

And in turn, I don't say anything when he unlaces his boots and shoves his jeans down.

Him standing in the middle of his room in nothing but black boxer briefs doesn't bring the same apprehension that it did the time he came out of the bathroom wrapped only in a towel.

So much has happened since then. I've had time to get used to the idea of him being more than someone who comforts me. I've had time to get to know him better. I've had time to accept that he'd never hurt me, not physically anyway. The rejection in the living room did sting more than I want to admit, if only so I don't give a voice to his ability to hurt my feelings.

He's not indifferent to me even in his silence. His eyes follow me everywhere. They stay on me when I disappear into his closet. They find me when I reemerge wearing nothing but one of his soft t-shirts. My hands tremble, and I want to explain that I'm not offering anything up to him, but the words don't seem necessary, not even when it's clear he can't take his eyes off my bare legs.

He ignores the length thickening between his thighs. His body has reactions to me all the time, but he's become an expert at ignoring it. We both have, honestly.

For all my bravado about wanting to confront him for not coming to me earlier, I keep my mouth clamped shut. I can sense that he wants to end things, even as his body responds to mine. I can tell he's not entirely comfortable with me in his room in only a shirt, even though at the same time, he's enjoying the view. He's torn just like I am.

He wants to touch me, and he wants to keep his distance.

He wants to ask me to leave, and yet he'll beg me to stay.

He wishes he'd never met me, and at the same time he can't imagine his life without me.

He's not looking for anything serious, yet he knows once with me would never be enough.

I'm nothing like the women he's been interested in before, and somehow, I'm all he's ever wanted.

I'm off-limits.

I'm broken.

I'll never be whole again.

Yet he's looking at me with half-lidded eyes and a desperation that's so thick it fills the room, swirling around us like fog in the wintertime. It's as if I'm the best and worst thing that's ever happened to him.

I circle him, trailing my fingers along the dips at his waist. Goosebumps pop up on his skin, but he remains silent. He doesn't reach for me or ask me to stop. He's a statue, a living breathing piece of art, and I take my time admiring him.

His breaths are rushing past his lips in rough pants of air, and mine are doing the same. I feel alive for the first time in as long as I can remember. I feel in control, and powerful, and the heady scent of his skin wraps all the way around me. He doesn't have to tell me I'm safe with him. I feel it deep in my bones. He doesn't have to tell me that what I'm doing is okay. I know it by the way his eyes beg me for more.

The only problem is, I don't have more to give. My body is singing, begging me to reach for his hand and put it on my skin, but at the same time, I know my limitations. Doing that would only make me shut down, so I let his arms hang by his sides.

I let a million things go unsaid. I let my lips linger against the soft skin of his back, even as he sucks in a harsh breath from the contact.

He still hasn't said a single word to me since he came home, and yet I feel as if we've had an hour-long conversation.

He still doesn't say anything when I clasp his hand in mine and urge him to get in the bed. He remains silent as I pull the covers over both of us and press my lips to his. He responds only by tightening his arm around me and holding me tight.

He doesn't deepen the kiss, and neither do I. He doesn't make promises or explain what happened while he was away. He doesn't flinch when I press my lips to each of his injuries. He doesn't make a joke about his erection needing attention when I nuzzle against him, making no effort to touch him further.

And he isn't in the bed when I wake in the morning.

Chapter 23

Scooter

Leaving her in my bed when I snuck out like a coward this morning was more difficult than I'd like to admit. Breathing in the fresh, cold air when I stepped onto the front porch of the clubhouse was the first full breath I took since I arrived home yesterday.

The dichotomy of emotions is enough to drive me crazy. She read me like an open book last night. I could see it in the way she watched me, the way she touched me like she never had before. She's well aware that I'm battling my own emotions but speaking about them out loud didn't seem fair. I'm not trying to convince her of anything one way or the other. She has to come to her own conclusions, figure out what she wants on her own without me trying to persuade her in a specific direction.

After this last trip, I don't even know which direction I want to go.

Frigid air bites my face as I ride my bike in the direction of the hospital. Kincaid wasn't joking about my evaluations, and he hit me with the news that it was happening today on the way back to the clubhouse yesterday afternoon.

I don't even have time to pause, time to take stock of what I feel or how I want things to turn out. I know I don't want to leave Cerberus and being forced out would leave a mark not only on my employment history but also on my sense of self. I don't want to be known as the man that would compromise his brothers for the sake of his own retribution, but that's how I'm being treated. Most of the guys have talked to me when I spoke to them, but none of them are open and willing to strike up a conversation with me themselves.

I'm nearly frozen solid and just grateful to be feeling something other than numb anger as I make it to the parking lot of the hospital. I have an eight o'clock appointment with Dr. Alverez on the fourth floor. I've been to her office before. Every potential Cerberus member travels to New Mexico prior to getting hired to undergo a battery of testing and interviews. They have to make sure that we're sane and capable of doing what is asked of us. They have to make sure that we're a good fit with the rest of the team before we sign our contract.

I have ten minutes to kill before my scheduled appointment, and I hate that I decided to quit smoking. It wasn't exactly a conscious decision, but I haven't gotten much of a chance since Mia came into my life. I never wanted to smell like smoke when she was against me, and we're always together.

I mark that under the pro column of my mental list of things where Mia's concerned and climb off my bike. Maybe if I get to the appointment early, I can get out of there faster.

My leather cut catches a few eyes as I walk across the parking lot, but no one scampers away. Cerberus is known to help people in this community, and even though most people stay out of our way, they aren't usually afraid of us either. Kincaid has spent decades fostering a relationship with many businesses in the area, and he takes pride in the positive reputation our club has.

The same disappointment I felt when Kincaid was talking to me in Venezuela weighs on my chest again, and I get the sense that people can see my shame as I walk inside. I receive a few nods, and one kid staring up at me the entire ride in the elevator, but no one says a word to me.

As usual, Dr. Alverez's office is silent as I enter. I check in with the receptionist, but before my ass can hit the chair in the waiting room, Dr. Alverez is walking toward me with her hand extended. Her grip is strong for such a small older lady, and I know from experience that she's a hard ass who doesn't have a problem calling grown men on their shit. It's why she's the best fit for Cerberus. I won't be able to bullshit her, but at the same time, minus the issues I have keeping Mia out of my thoughts while I'm working, I don't have any problems.

Let's see if Dr. Alverez comes to the same conclusion.

Testing lasts all day. She starts with an IQ test, which is ridiculous. I think she only does it to make me feel stupid or to piss me off so I flounder on the other tests. After a fifteen-minute break, where I spend the entire time pacing around a small room wondering how I got so bad at math since my last IQ test, she shows me to a small room and gives me a personality test.

This test is nothing like those stupid quizzes in a women's magazine. I'm talking about over five hundred questions meant to really pick apart my brain and check for psychopathy, and since I entered the test already agitated from the IQ test, I'm now certain Dr. Alverez has it out for me, which only makes me want to answer the questions with how I'm feeling right at this moment. I may end up in a padded room before the day is out, and that's even worse than ending up in prison for shooting Agent Butler without hesitation.

When I'm done, Dr. Alverez comes into the room smiling like a fool as she takes a seat across from me.

"Really?" I ask when she holds up a card the size of a piece of notebook paper.

She cuts her eyes to the card and back to me.

"Butterfly," I mutter, feeling ridiculous.

She lays that card down and shows me the next.

"Butterfly," I mutter again.

"I need you to take this seriously, Mr. Gabhart."

"I didn't know the psychiatric community even used Rorschach anymore."

"We use lots of things. What do you see?"

"A gorilla?"

We go through the black and white and the colored inkblots, and every time she jots something down on the paper beside her, the crazier I feel. Just when I think it'll never be over, she asks me to wait in her office while she compiles some scores.

I feel like this is another test. She has numerous manipulatives on her bookcases, things she may use when treating children, and even as tempted as I am to go pick them up, I sit statute-still in the chair across from her desk.

It seems like an eternity before her office door opens and she walks in.

She doesn't say a word as she takes the seat behind her desk and rifles through some paperwork.

I'm the first one to speak up. "Am I crazy, Doc? Unfit for duty?"

There's humor in my voice, but I don't find anything funny about today at all.

It's clear she doesn't either when she glances up and gives me a chastising look. It's reminiscent of the way my own mother would look at me when I did something stupid as a kid.

"Tell me about Mia."

You could hear a pin drop in the room as I stare at her.

"I'm here for psych testing not a therapy session."

Finding what she's looking for, she jots a few notes down, covering the notebook back up when I angle my head to see what she's writing. This is psychological warfare at its finest, and if I were in a better headspace right now, I might actually find it a little comical. Only there isn't a damn thing funny about being here. My career with Cerberus depends on the outcome of today.

"You're here so I can determine if you're fit to return to work after your suspension is over," she clarifies. "Tell me about Mia."

I clamp my jaw shut, unsure if she just wants the macro details of how I know Mia or if she's interested in knowing that I've pretty much named myself her champion and protector.

"Take your time," she says with a soothing voice. "I cleared my schedule for today."

The last part is a warning. She's letting me know that stall tactics won't work. We'll be here until the sun rises tomorrow if that's how long it takes.

I narrow my eyes at her, but she doesn't look back at me with smugness. It's a battle of wills that she knows she's going to win, and clearly, she's got the patience of a saint.

Sighing, I settle further into my chair, just barely staving off asking her if I should lie down to be analyzed. I don't think humor will earn me any points, not considering the gravity of the situation that brought me here today.

"I pulled Mia out of a compound in Miami right before Christmas. She'd been in captivity for seven weeks." I close my mouth again, looking at the doctor and deciding what I can tell her. "This isn't my story."

"This *is* your story," she says as she drops her pen. "This is about what Mia is to you. Tell me about the things as they pertain to Ryan Gabhart. You aren't betraying her trust. If you hurt because she was hurt, that's what we talk about. If you're angry because of what happened to her, that's what we discuss. This is *your* story."

In what seems like one long breath, I tell Dr. Alverez everything.

I tell her about Mia's attachment to me, and how it not only makes me feel useful but scares me because I'm terrified of being responsible for her mental health recovery.

I confess my fears of losing her, and my fears of loving her, of pushing too hard and not pushing enough.

I speak of my distractions and my need for blood from the men that hurt her. I explain that even though they're dead, I still don't feel like Mia was avenged to the magnitude she deserves.

I confide my disappointment in myself for the way I handled things on our last mission, letting her know that although in the moment my life wasn't a concern, putting Jinx at risk isn't something I'll forgive myself for anytime soon.

I bat at the angry tears streaming down my face when I realize that caring for Mia may cost me what I've loved most about my life, but also acknowledging that Cerberus was only meant to be a steppingstone until I got bored. Yet, I've been with them for years, re-signed my contract twice already, and I've never questioned leaving before. I tell her I don't want to leave now.

I also admit that my distractions stem mainly from not knowing where I stand with the woman whom I share a bed with every night. It's the uncertainties that plague me. It's the doubts and fears that keep me from being able to compartmentalize my life the way Kincaid insisted that I need to.

When I walk out of her office, I feel somehow lighter and even more burdened, so I don't go back to the clubhouse immediately. I don't call Mia on the phone and discuss things like a damn adult as Dr. Alverez instructed.

I jump on my bike and ride around until I can no longer feel my face or my fingertips.

Chapter 24

Mia

He held me all night last night, yet it still felt like goodbye.

Without a word of rejection, he asked me to leave by not asking me to stay.

When I found his side of the bed cold and empty, I got up myself with renewed determination.

Broken isn't sexy.

Broken takes too much time to heal.

Broken isn't worth the time.

I pack the things Jasmine brought for me right back into the bag she used, leaving the handgun in the bedside table and text Max.

Mia: I need a plane ticket home.

Max: Dates?

Mia: Now. Today, please.

Max: What's going on?

He doesn't give me time to respond before my phone is lighting up with his name. I send him to voicemail, not trusting my voice to carry a conversation.

Mia: Just get me the ticket, please.

I grab a quick shower, hoping I can get out of here before Ryan returns. He avoided me for hours yesterday, and I don't expect today to be any different.

By the time I've showered and gotten dressed there's a text from Max on my phone telling me that he's gotten me a plane ticket and he's on his way to pick me up to take me to the airport.

He asks a million questions when he first arrives but grows silent ten minutes into the hour drive to Durango when he realizes that I'm not going to answer a single one.

I'm adding my deceptive twin brother to the list of people I need to have long, hard conversations with, but today isn't his day. Today and for however long it takes, I face my demons in Louisiana.

He parks the SUV he borrowed from Kingston and insists on walking me to the security checkpoint. I don't argue with him, and honestly it takes everything I have not to ask him to accompany me all the way back to Louisiana.

"Ma and Pa will be at the airport to pick you up," he tells me as he pulls the strap of my duffel bag off his shoulder.

I take the strap, shouldering the weight, and really look at my brother for the first time since I was rescued. He's older than I remember, my memories from over ten years ago still trying to accept this new man in front of me.

"Thank you," I tell him.

He lifts his arms like he wants to hug me, and I really need that from him, but his arms drop as a weak smile tugs up the corners of his mouth.

"Be safe," he says as he takes a step back. "Text me and let me know when you land, and also when Ma and Pa find you."

I nod my agreement, but I have to turn around and walk away when I feel tears burning the back of my eyes. If I start crying now, I know I'll never stop, and I don't think United would let a hysterical woman on their plane.

I make it through security without issue, and even though I'm starving, I arrow to my gate, unable to stand in a food line with people behind me. I find a quiet corner at the empty gate across from mine and settle in. My phone burns in my back pocket with the need to text Ryan and tell him where I am, but I'm sure Max will give him all the details. What scares me the most, what keeps me from reaching out to him is fear of hearing relief in his voice when I tell him that I'm going home. I've impeded on his life too much as it is, but it doesn't stop me from missing him. It's only been twelve hours since I've seen his face, but it feels like a million years.

The plane ride is smooth, other than the shaky takeoff and landing, and I mentally commend myself for handling it as well as I did while I walk through the New Orleans airport. My face is stoic, and I refuse to look anyone in the eye as I make my way to the pickup area. I fell for a smiling face once, and I'll never make that mistake again, even if it means sacrificing pleasantries and common courtesy.

Airport traffic is thankfully calm, most people having traveled for the holidays are already back home and working on this Wednesday afternoon.

I fake a smile when I see my mother waiting by the curb when I exit.

"Where's Pa?"

People swarm around us, and I should feel safe in public, but I don't. Any one of the people walking around us could mean to do us harm, so I press my back to one of the huge concrete pillars and keep a vigilant eye on the crowd.

"He had to drive around. I got out because I didn't want to miss you," she explains.

I want to scoff and tell her that it's not like I'd leave with someone else if they weren't there the second I walked outside, but I can see her actions for the blessing that they are. The old me would've called her crazy, but the old me hadn't been taken and tortured for seven weeks.

"Thank you," I tell her.

She wraps her arms around me, and as much as I want to sink into her embrace, I keep my eyes open, all the time wondering what I look like to strangers. Most likely they see me as an unappreciative asshole. I know I would've thought that if I saw a daughter getting hugged by a loved one who is looking anywhere but at the one with her arms around them.

I smile down at her for a brief moment when she steps back and brushes something off the shoulder of my jacket.

My dad pulls up to the curb and blares the horn. I know he thinks that acting impatient and hustling us along will look good to the airport security guard directing traffic and making sure people aren't sitting and waiting for their passengers to step outside. He's been a United States citizen for decades, but he still fears that ICE will pop out of nowhere and cart him back to Mexico.

An unplanned smile stretches across my face when my mother mutters curse words about impatient men under her breath. My dad's thumbs are tapping on the steering wheel as we climb inside, and I know every other second, he's darting his eyes toward the security guard. I chuckle as I belt myself in, knowing he won't pull away until we're all obeying the law.

If only his diligence had kept me from being taken.

I clear my throat, pushing thoughts like that away.

I want to do what Ryan insisted in our first conversation before the last raids. I want to fully forgive myself. I want to truly believe that getting taken wasn't my fault, but I know that's going to take more time.

"Gonna drop you and Ma off at the house and then I'll go grocery shopping. We didn't have time to get all of your favorite foods. This was an unexpected visit," my dad says, never taking his eyes off the road.

"I'd like to go to my apartment first," I tell him as I watch other cars zip past us, going at least ten miles over the speed limit.

"Oh," Mom snaps. "We forgot to tell Jason you were coming."

I start to tell her that she doesn't need to, but her fingers are working over the keys on her cell phone like she was born with it in her hands.

It's only a ten-minute drive to the apartment I shared with Jason, and I insist they stay in the car while I go up to grab a few things. I realize my mistake when I get to the third floor. I don't have keys. I didn't even have my ID when I was found, but somehow, I ended up with a new copy. The only cash I have is what Max shoved in my hand before we went inside the Durango airport.

Taking my chances, even though it's still too early for Jason to be home, I lift my hand and knock.

Surprisingly the door swings up. Only it's a woman with a smile melting from her face instead of Jason.

She's gorgeous with long blonde hair and bright blue eyes, and she's clearly comfortable in this space because she's not wearing shoes.

"Mia?"

My brows draw together when she says my name. How does she know my name when I've never seen her before in my life, and that's saying something because Jason and I have been together for many years?

"Is Jason home?" I'm surprised when no emotion marks my tone.

I feel nothing standing here looking at her in what I used to consider my own home.

"He's not back from work yet," she says as she steps to the side. "Please come in."

I waiver for a while, not sure if I'd be safe closed in the apartment alone with her, but I shove it all down and step inside anyway.

The TV plays a sitcom in the background as I walk into the living room. She lives here with him, and that's clear from the change in décor. There's a woman's touch here that is different from my own.

"I'm Cynthia," she says as she holds her hand out.

I take it, shaking it like a normal person does when a hand is offered, but inside my mind is spinning wondering why I don't care that she's in my space, and then it dawns on me. This isn't my space. It hasn't been for months.

But this does explain why Jason was so eager to get home when I was hospitalized.

"Mia, but you already know that."

She gives me a weak, guilty smile.

"I'm here to get my things," I tell her.

A relieved breath escapes her lips, and the tension drawing up her shoulders flows away. I know she was anticipating a fight or argument, but there's nothing here, including Jason, worth fighting for.

"Your things are in here."

I follow Cynthia to the guest bedroom, grateful that my belongings are packed neatly away in plastic containers rather than trash bags. It's clear she packed them because Jason wouldn't have bothered to fold my clothes neatly or wrap my breakable items in bubble wrap.

"Thank you for taking such great care with my things," I tell her.

"I feel like I owe you an explanation."

"Did you know we were together when you started dating?"

Her head shakes back and forth.

"I didn't know until they—until you were—I didn't know until he had to fly to Miami." She swallows and when tears form in the corner of her eyes, I know she's about to deliver a blow. "He told me you were dead. He asked me for help with packing your things because it was too hard for him to do it alone."

"You deserve better," I tell her without emotion.

"I just—" I hold my hand up to keep the excuses from slipping past her lips.

"You don't owe me anything, but I'd be grateful if you could help me get some of these things down to my dad's car." I hold up my cast in explanation.

"Of course."

"Just the clothing for now. I'll get my dad to swing by some other time for the rest."

I'm able to help by grabbing the handle of my rolling suitcase. I don't have a clue what's in it, but since I don't want to be helpless, I drag it behind me while she carries one of the plastic totes.

Thankfully, neither one of my parents say a word as the stranger helps me load my things in the trunk.

Cynthia is heading back inside to grab one more container since there's room in the trunk when Jason whips into the parking lot. His truck rocks back and forth because he slammed it in park before he even stopped moving.

"Mia!" He runs to me, wrapping his arms around me in an embrace that doesn't even hold an ounce of the comfort I feel when Ryan does the same. "Oh, God, baby. I'm so glad you're home."

"I'm not home, Jason." I wiggle out of his arms, pressing my palm to his chest to get the distance I need. "You're home."

"But—"

I angle my head in Cynthia's direction as she watches her boyfriend or whatever he is to her look at me like I'm the long-lost love of his life.

"She's home."

His face pales when he realizes that I've already been inside and met her.

"This isn't my home." As I say the words, I realize that I'm referring to Louisiana as a whole.

"We can work through this," he insists, pushing his chest against my hand to get closer to me. "I'll never love another woman the way I love you."

I don't have a damn clue why he's fighting for what we had when it was dead long before he ever gave his current girlfriend some sob story about me dying. He gave up on me long before my hope for him faded with the setting sun after weeks in Miami.

"It's over, Jason."

"Mia," he sighs, his head hanging low between his shoulders, and I can't help but sense relief coming from him as well.

Maybe he feels like he has to act a certain way because of everything that has happened, but he's off the hook for all of it because I just can't find the energy to care.

He watches as I close the trunk and nods his head in understanding when I let him know that my dad will be by soon to get the rest of my things.

He doesn't say another word or beg me to stay when I climb inside the car. He merely nods like he's grateful everything went as smoothly with me as it did. When I look up at Cynthia as my dad pulls away, I can tell by the look on her face that things won't be as simple with her. That makes a genuine smile spread across my face.

Chapter 25

Scooter

Agitation with myself kept me away until well after the sun set.

But my draw to her brought me back, just like I know it always will.

She's in my blood, so deep in my soul that staying away from her isn't an option.

I don't think I'll ever regain blood flow in my hands from being out so long in the dead of winter, but I hope a quick shower and lying with her in the bed will thaw me out.

The clubhouse is a little rowdy when I step inside. The guys are always looking for a good time, especially after being gone for a couple days. Music plays through the speakers as a few women from town dance near the sofas.

I don't see Mia, but it seems the booze is flowing, and I know she'd never be out here with all of that going on.

I head straight for my room. I've already been away from her long enough, and I have a ton of explaining to do. I have a million questions that need answering, and a slew of confessions I need to make to her.

"She's gone," Max says as I pass by Kingston's room on the way to my own.

I stop in my tracks and back up. Jasmine is sitting on the bed as Kingston packs his things into cardboard boxes. Max is stationed in the recliner by the window.

"What was that?" I ask, certain he didn't just say what I thought he did.

"Mia is gone."

"Gone shopping? Gone to the doctor?"

"Gone home. Back to Louisiana."

I want to chuckle and call him an asshole for trying to get me riled up, but it's clear by the look on his face that he isn't joking.

"What happened?" She was sleeping soundly when I left this morning.

"I was going to ask you the same thing." His voice is just short of a growl, and it's filled with accusation. "She wouldn't talk to me today. She just insisted I get her back home, today."

"You put her on a plane alone?" I hiss. "Are you fucking crazy?"

My heart rate doubles, and it's taking all my power not to cross the room and knock his fucking head off.

Kingston steps out of the bedroom and challenges me with a single look. Without words, he's telling me that if I move on his man, he'll move on me.

I don't back down because of fear. I can hold my own against Kingston "Tug" Jacks, but I don't engage because I know Mia enough to know that my silence last night drove her away. Her head is filling with all sorts of misplaced thoughts about me not wanting her, me not needing her, me not caring for her. She's thinking she's a burden like she's felt in the past.

"She made it home safely," Max offers, and I'm thankful he's given me this nugget of information when it's clear he isn't going to spare me much else. "She's with my parents."

Does that mean she didn't go home to *him*?

Not necessarily, and that thought hits me in the chest like a wrecking ball.

"You moving out, man?" I turn my attention to Tug, since I don't know what to do with the information given to me.

I'm on lockdown orders while suspended, unable to leave town. It's not a time to go and do what I want. If I head to Louisiana to get her back, I'll lose my job with Cerberus. It's a breach of contract, and automatic dismissal. My suspension isn't a vacation. It's meant to be a time of reflection and introspection, an adult version of a timeout so to speak.

"Figured I'm not staying here much anyway. Kincaid asked me to clean out my room. I think he's got someone new coming in," Tug answers as he shoves a pile of jeans in a box.

Jasmine huffs and shoos him out of the way. She reaches in the box and removes the pile of clothes before refolding each pair of jeans and placing them back inside. Tug pinches her ass. Jasmine squeals, and Max smiles at their antics.

I don't feel like joining in on their playfulness, so I walk away. I can't go to my room. I don't want to see it empty. I don't want the visual reminder that she took off.

I head in the opposite direction, straight to the bar. Grinch sees me coming and pours a glass for me while he's topping off his own.

"Thanks, man," I mutter before bringing the heavy glass to my lips.

He nods, and I expect him to scurry away, since that's what most of the guys have been doing since shit went down in Venezuela, but he stands there beside me drinking and taking in the crowd. It's not too crazy. It's not even close to some of the parties we have here, but I know it'll only grow. If we—if they—don't get orders to head out for another job, this place will be packed come Friday night, and things will be even crazier once the guys realize that Mia isn't here.

What she doesn't know is that every one of them have kept things as chill as possible since she arrived. They respect her need to heal in a calm environment, and she's got no clue that the Cerberus clubhouse, usually is never calm and peaceful. The guys find tranquility in willing women, loud music, and enough alcohol to make them forget about the things they've done and seen. We live our lives to the fullest, one party, one sexed-up night at a time until the orders come down that we're heading out. Then we're all business.

Grinch drains his glass, and I swallow what's left of mine so he can refill it when he pours himself another one.

"Surprised you're out here," Grinch says as he screws the lid back on the whiskey.

"She's gone." I know what he's hinting at, so there's no sense in beating around the bush.

"Gone?" He repositions, standing in front of me and blocking my view of the rowdy crowd.

"Back to Louisiana." I clench my jaw.

"For good?"

I shrug my shoulders. "No clue."

I turn the glass up and drain it for the second time in less than ten minutes. I'm not going to feel anything very soon, but I know I'm going to regret this in the morning.

Other than an occasional beer, I haven't drunk much in the last month. My tolerance has taken a nosedive in such a short time, I question my reasoning for a third as Grinch pours us both another.

"I know why I'm drinking like this," I mutter as I look up at him. "Why are you drinking like the weight of the world is on your shoulders?"

He shrugs. "Got bad news from home."

"Fucking sucks." I tap my glass against his in solidarity, and we both chug.

We're five glasses in when he spots something he says will make him feel better. That something is about five feet tall and has red hair down to her ass. I chuckle as he walks away, but the laughter falls from my lips as I watch Kirsty walk toward me with a seductive sway in her hips.

"Hey there, stranger," she coos as she gets close enough that I can hear her over the din of the music.

I catch her wrist before she can drag her red fingernail down my chest.

"It's not nice to touch people without permission," I chastise.

A lazy grin tugs up the corners of her lips. "Is that how we're playing it?"

Her eyes sparkle as she takes in my face, and I know she can tell I'm drunk. She's seen it enough times to recognize the cues, and it's also clear that she isn't concerned that I haven't called or stopped by her place in over a month. Kirsty's a free-loving woman. She wasn't the only chick I spent time with before, and I wasn't the only man to warm her bed in recent months either.

"Do I need to ask permission to suck your cock, too?"

She makes like she's going to hit her knees right here in the middle of the clubhouse living room, but I grab her hip with my free hand before she can lower herself to the floor. I wouldn't put it past her to give me head in view of everyone. I've seen her do it before. Jinx is into a little public sex, but it's never been my thing.

"You're wasting your time, Kirsty."

"So, you just want to jump straight to fucking me in the ass?"

In another lifetime, my cock would stiffen with her words, the suggestion of letting me in her ass, and the seductive way she licks her lips, but things have changed drastically over the last several weeks. She doesn't appeal to me at all. Emotionless sex doesn't carry the same thrill it once did.

"We had a good time." She nods her head, too intoxicated to sense where this conversation is going. I stand from the stool in front of the bar and back away from her. She tries to step closer, taking it as an invitation to join me, but I hold both hands up to stop her. "It was fun, but that's all it was, and whatever it was, it's over now."

Her eyes narrow, but it's with confusion rather than animosity. "You sure?"

"One hundred percent," I tell her with an overexaggerated nod. "Have a good night."

She shrugs, much like I figured she would and walks back to the group of guys near the pool table.

When I turn back around, finally ready to face my empty room, I run right into Max's chest.

"You surprised me, Scooter."

I take a step back, only now realizing how unsteady I am on my own two feet.

"Surprised?" I slur. I felt sober as a church mouse while I was sitting, but it's like the alcohol just hit me.

"Your turning her away isn't exactly how I saw you reacting to that woman."

I huff, my eyes closing on a slow blink that takes more power than it should to reopen them. "Men in love don't go looking for cheap thrills."

I walk past him, praying I can make it to my fucking bed before I pass out when I hear him mutter, "Indeed they don't."

My sheets still smell like her pear body wash, and I don't bother kicking my shoes off as I crash onto my mattress and bury my face into the pillows. I'm not giving up on her. I'm not giving up on us, but I will give her time to figure out that here with me is exactly where she needs to be.

Chapter 26

Mia

I'm regretting my decision as I sit in the corner booth of the diner and shred another napkin. The first three are in a neat little pile near my empty coffee cup. It's not empty because of poor service. I turned the waitress away the last time she stopped by. I've had two cups already on top of what I drank at my parents' house this morning, and I'm feeling like I should go out and run a marathon, which is alarming because I loathe running. Always have, and I don't see that changing anytime soon.

My head fills with memories as I watch Jason walk toward me. He was once the man of my dreams, the smiling handsome man who had goals and dreams that we often spoke about accomplishing together. While he was still in law school and we had our whole lives in front of us, we'd lie in bed and whisper our plans to one another. We'd spend entire weekends together, never really getting out of bed unless it was to eat or shower the sweat from our bodies after hours of lovemaking. I remember running my fingers through his hair and watching his eyes flutter closed with the contact.

And even as hard as I try, I can't pinpoint the exact moment when things changed. I don't even know if there was an exact second in time that he became someone I no longer recognized. Maybe it was a gradual transition once he got hired at the law firm. Maybe he saw what others had, and since he was never willing to put in the same amount of work, he became bitter and entitled. None of it matters now. These are his and Cynthia's problems to contend with.

Jason isn't smiling now, and his eyes are circled with exhaustion, the normally vibrant skin a sickly dull color. It's clear he didn't get much sleep last night, and I can already predict how this conversation is going to go before he takes a seat across from me.

He holds his hand up and snaps his fingers to get the waitress's attention before he even greets me.

Has he always behaved this way? Was I blind to his blatant level of disrespect for others?

My parents told me they didn't have a clue that Jason had moved another woman into our apartment. My mother sobbed for over an hour last night when I explained who the woman was that helped me get my things in the car. She's more distraught than I am over the dissolution of our relationship. I never confessed the decline in our relationship with my parents. I figured if I hadn't made a plan to leave him, then complaining about something I was tolerating was unnecessary.

Like any good man, my father wanted to go to his house and beat the crap out of him, but I reminded him that doing so would be illegal, and he backed down rather quickly. I explained things then, letting them know that I was unhappy long before I was abducted. Ma's tears began to dry, but Pa spent the remainder of the evening consoling her and reminding me how strong and beautiful I am, and that I don't need a man to be whole.

This isn't something new to me. My father has always urged me to be independent. I think that's why I'm in my early thirties and still haven't gotten married yet. It's why I knew deep down that I'd never take the next step to spend the rest of my life with a man like Jason.

I didn't explain my feelings for Ryan simply because I don't completely understand them myself.

As I watch Jason chastise the waitress for overfilling his coffee cup, I can't help feeling relief over dodging this bullet. It still doesn't keep me from criticizing myself to agreeing to meet him today, though. I should've left well enough alone, but after he called my parents' house incessantly this morning, I gave in, capitulating to a final meeting before I wash my hands of him for good.

"What did you want to discuss?"

He looks up from his coffee as if he's annoyed that I'm sitting here in front of him when he's the one who suggested we meet, and it takes a lot of control to keep my lip from twitching with how funny it is to me now, how easy it is to take a step back and see his true colors.

He watches me for a few long moments, and I want to shy away when his eyes dart to the scarf covering my shaved head. I know he saw the damage that was done to my hair before he took off from Miami, and the look on his face tells me that he sees me as less than a woman. It's what I felt as Ryan used the clippers to trim away the long tresses. Only now I stiffen my spine rather than give into the burn of tears behind my eyes.

"You look like a cancer patient," he says as he tilts his head to the side, and I can see the wheels turning in his own head. He's trying to figure out a way to take advantage of this entire situation, to use my tragedy to gain a higher foothold for himself.

I want to kick myself for being so blind to his arrogance, egotism, and narcissism for so long. This man is toxic. He's a controlling coward, and although he's never raised a hand to strike me, I don't doubt that he would, eventually. He'd have no other recourse when the words he used as weapons were no longer effective.

"Any other snide comments you feel like making about my appearance?" I snap, my lip twitching in irritation now rather than humor.

His eyes fill with fake sympathy as he reaches across the table to clasp my hands. I pull them back and place them in my lap, refusing to let him touch me.

"Cynthia left me." He says this with as much emotion as I feel toward him right now, which is a tablespoon short of a teaspoon.

I don't respond to him, but on the inside, I'm throwing that woman a party all the while praying for the sanity of the next girl he lures in with his bright eyes and winning smile.

"I miss you, and I want us to work things out."

I scoff at his declaration.

"You don't miss me. You need someone to be at your beck and call. You want someone to be waiting for you when you get home like they can't breathe until you arrive and chip them off a little piece of your attention. You want a maid and a cook, and someone to rant to when you've been overlooked for another promotion by the person who always works harder than you. You want someone to agree with you when you complain about being discriminated against even though you're nothing more than an entitled, wealthy, white man who doesn't understand the privileges afforded to him just by breathing air."

Jason looks at me with his jaw hanging slightly open, but he doesn't make a sound. He doesn't argue or counter my claims. I think I've stunned him. I've never said such things to him, never stood up for myself or put his own flaws on display the way he did to me so readily and often.

"You don't want me, Jason, and things haven't been good between us for a long time."

"You promised to marry me," he finally mutters. "You agreed to be my wife."

"You put me on the spot in the middle of your company's Fourth of July bash. That wasn't for me. It was for a show, another way for you to be the center of attention among your bosses and coworkers."

"You said yes."

"I regretted it the second the word fell from my lips."

"You love me."

"I *loved* you," I clarify. "And that love died long ago."

"Is this because of him?"

I don't even have to ask who he's talking about. He's well aware of where I've been the last couple of weeks.

"This is because you're bitter, and hateful. This is because I deserve more than you'll ever have to offer. You need to work on yourself and your own character flaws before you can even begin to be truly happy or make someone feel loved by you. I'm not arm candy. I'm not invisible except for the times when showing me off benefits you."

He doesn't have a rebuttal as I stand.

"Goodbye, Jason."

A couple of women clap as I leave the diner, and my cheeks flush as I realize my voice had gotten louder and louder as I continued to speak to him. Pride fills my chest as I walk to the parking lot to climb into my dad's waiting car. I feel invincible. I feel powerful, and I can finally breathe deep without choking on that freedom.

"Where to, *mija*?" Dad asks as he waits for me to put my seatbelt on.

"To the mall. I have some demons to concur."

Chapter 27

Scooter

Two weeks of silence.

Two weeks of misery.

Two weeks of utter boredom.

My will to give Mia space is running dry.

At night I toss and turn, wondering if she's back in his arms. Max feeds me morsels of information, and I eat them up like a starving child, but it doesn't keep my mind from taking over and running wild.

He said she and Jason are over, but he didn't give me anymore information than that. I can't help but wonder if Jason is wooing her, begging her to take him back. It's what I would do. I don't think I could take no from her lips as a final answer. I'd do anything in my power to win her back.

Cerberus left three days ago on a mission to South Africa, and even though I'm still under clubhouse arrest for lack of a better description, Kincaid didn't exclude me from the meetings when they were gearing up to go.

The good news is that the CIA has no plans to bring formal charges against me for shooting Gabriella Butler. They aren't very happy about not being able to interrogate her, but as it turns out both Jiménez and the Cortez brothers were astute businessmen. They ran their sex trafficking organization the way most fortune five hundred companies operated, and that meant there were a ton of documentation and evidence left behind. They killed the women but didn't burn the records and money lines. Cerberus has jobs lined up for months, not to bring a specific woman home, but missions to continue cutting the heads off snakes.

South America has been a hotbed for the illegal sex trade for decades, but South Africa is also a hub of activity, and according to the confiscated records, that's where the Cortezs' were shipping many of their women off to.

"She's okay," Jasmine whispers when Max heads to the kitchen to grab them a snack.

Her phone pings another text message, and Dominic's daughter smiles down at her phone.

"You're texting with her right now?" I ask, excitement filling my blood and making me feel alive for the first time in the last two weeks. "Let me see."

She glares at me as she clutches her phone to her chest. "Not likely."

"What time does the game start?" Max asks as he comes back carrying two different kinds of chips and a jar of baby dill pickles.

Jasmine scoffs. "Like I freaking know."

"Kingston may be gone right now, but that doesn't mean I won't spank that pretty little ass of yours," he whispers too loudly in her ear.

Jasmine's eyes find mine, and her cheeks flush red with embarrassment when she realizes that I heard what her man just said to her. I don't understand the dynamic between the three of them, but it works for them. Her dad seems okay with it, so I don't have an opinion, not that I would if Dominic was opposed. I'm all for grown people doing what makes them happy so long as they don't hurt anyone else.

"Still got fifteen minutes," I mutter as I look down at the empty screen of my own cell phone.

I should text her, but the possibility that she may not text me back, combined with the fact that she's clearly texting Jasmine would kill me. Her being too busy to respond is one thing. Outright ignoring me would put me in a headspace I don't think I'd handle very well right now.

The TV is on, but none of us are watching it. Max and I are both watching Jasmine for totally different reasons, and she's focused on the cell phone in her hand. I wonder how fast Max's reflexes are, and if he's armed. I'm contemplating snatching her phone just to see what Mia has texted her over the last two weeks, but before I commit, my own cell phone chimes.

My elated heart nearly thuds to a stop when I see that Kirsty has sent a message not Mia.

I block her number without even reading the entire message. Clearly, she didn't get the message weeks ago at the party, and I don't have the patience to explain to a now sober Kirsty what I said when she was drunk. She's at the clubhouse too often for it to be the last time I'll run into her. I just hope that she gets the hint that I'm not interested between now and the next time.

A second run-in won't be as pleasant for her. Just a phone call between Kirsty and I sent Mia out of this clubhouse into the freezing weather. She could've ended up hurt or worse that night. I won't risk hurting her, even indirectly, ever again. I don't want passing looks or flirtations to be misconstrued by the girl I'm planning to convince to spend her life with me. If that means living like a monk and cutting all ties from every other chick who graced my bed, then so be it.

"Turn up the volume," Max urges when Jasmine's phone pings over and over.

"Calm down," she tells him with a bright smile on her face. "The game hasn't even started yet."

He gives her a look of warning, but all it does is make her blush and squirm in her seat. I have no doubt that the headboard in Kingston's old room will be slamming against our shared wall tonight. Just what I need is an auditory reminder of what I haven't had since long before Christmas.

It's not that I even miss sex. Yeah, I want to do everything under the sun with Mia when she's ready, but I miss her body heat, her head on my chest, and the soft whisper of her breath on my skin as she sleeps. If I had that from her for the rest of my life, I could die a happy man.

"What's got you so twisted up, man?"

I don't even bother looking over at Max. He knows exactly what's wrong with me, and I don't think he's taunting me, but until he saw me turn Kirsty down after getting the news that Mia had left, he hated my guts. His sister clung to me for comfort rather than him, and I know that ate him alive. He sees me do one decent thing, and all of a sudden, we're best pals? Hardly.

I wouldn't even be in the living room with these two lovebirds if my room wasn't closing in on me. I've always wanted to be a part of a team. It's why I played football in high school and why I joined the Marine Corps. It's why Cerberus is so appealing to me.

There's nothing worse than feeling lonely even when you're around other people, and I've had more than my fair share over the last two weeks. At least Jinx was talking to me again before they left for South Africa. We haven't really sat down and had a heart-to-heart about what happened, but at least he doesn't walk out of the room when I speak to him now. I disappointed all the guys, but Jinx, being the one in the room with me with a bird's-eye view of the way I treated Jiménez was hit the hardest.

I lost a lot of their respect, and I know it's going to be a struggle for them to trust me again if I'm ever allowed back out in the field with them. I'll work my ass off for that to happen. I'm not ready to give up on Cerberus, and I pray they haven't given up on me either.

The game finally starts, and even with as much enthusiasm as Max had to watch this game, he seems to only be able to concentrate on Jasmine. I understand everything about that, though. If Mia were here, I wouldn't be able to focus on anything but her either.

The sound of a car outside draws my attention, but neither Max nor Jasmine seem concerned. The clubhouse is the only thing on this stretch of road, and it ends in a dead-end less than a mile past, with all property on either side belonging to Cerberus.

It's not unheard of for people to get turned around or to drive by to get a look at the clubhouse, so I stand from the sofa and make my way to the front door, praying it isn't a group of people looking for a party. We never announce when we're gone because we know that the women are here mostly alone, and that means people will occasionally stop by to see if the lot is filled.

It isn't a lost car, but a taxi that's idling at the front of the property. When I look back at Jasmine, she has a sly look on her pretty face, and it only serves to ramp up my heart rate as I wait to see who is climbing out of the car.

Chapter 28

Mia

The plane ride home was even easier for me to deal with than the one I flew out on two weeks ago.

Fourteen days doesn't seem like a long period of time, but for me, those days were life changing.

The cabbie doesn't seem impressed that I'm just sitting in the car looking at the front of the clubhouse as he glares at me in the rearview mirror, but other than a loud sigh, he hasn't told me to get out.

I'm not waffling between staying or leaving. I know I'm getting out of this car, but it's what happens after that keeps me glued to the seat for a few minutes longer.

I don't have to wait long to see how I'll react to seeing Ryan again after what has seemed like forever because he opens the front door and stands on the threshold. Jasmine knew I was coming, but I begged her not to tell anyone. I'm sure Max knows because she doesn't keep anything from him, but from the look on Ryan's face as he tries to determine who's in the cab, she kept the news from him.

"Lady?" the cabbie finally grunts. "Are we staying or are we leaving?"

I don't fault the man for wanting to get on his way, but I'm also mildly annoyed that he's rushing my moment. Doesn't he know how important this little slice of time is? Of course he doesn't, and why should he? I was silent the entire drive from the airport, and he's now over an hour away from his normal area. I swipe my debit card through the reader and open the cab door.

Pulling the handle of the single suitcase I traveled with behind me, I climb out of the cab, never taking my eyes off of Ryan. His face is unreadable. He doesn't rush off the front porch and swing me around in his arms like I imagined. He doesn't frown and yell like the other scenario I created in my head. He just stands there, impassive as the cab drives away, leaving me standing in the parking lot immediately questioning if I made the right or wrong decision.

"Emmalyn said I was welcome back," I tell him.

He doesn't answer me, but that strong jaw of his tenses in response. I want to run my fingers down his face, brush my lips against his, confess everything I've been too scared to admit to myself until very recently.

I do none of those things, however. I shuffle my feet, piling the pea gravel with the tip of my boot and try to figure out what my next move is going to be.

Cold air swirls around me, the ends of the scarf wrapped around my head fluttering in the breeze. I probably look a hot mess. The decision to come back here was just as hasty as the one when I chose to leave. I didn't think it through, although I've known for days that this is where I want to be.

He hasn't texted or called. He hasn't tried to reach out at all, but neither have I. It's not that I didn't want to. I just knew I had to work through some serious things before I could concentrate on what I left behind, and as I stand here and watch his hands twitch at his sides, I wonder if that was the wrong move. Maybe I should've explained, or left a note before leaving, but at the time I didn't know what was waiting for me in Louisiana. I didn't know leaving Jason for good was going to be so easy and cathartic. I didn't know that I'd find my strength and ability to persevere in the middle of the second night I tried to sleep at my parents' house.

"It's cold," Ryan grunts. "Get inside."

I nod, walking toward him with my small suitcase bumping along the gravel as I make my way toward him. He doesn't stop in the living room once we enter. He heads for the hallway, and unlike the last time when I kept my distance when he ignored me, I follow right behind him, merely offering a quick wave to Jasmine and Max in the living room.

He's sitting on his bed when I get to his room, and as not to be presumptuous, I leave my suitcase in the hall near the door and join him inside.

"Have a nice trip?" His words are mumbled as he stares down at his hands as if they hold all his secrets.

"I went straight from the airport to the apartment I shared with Jason."

He tenses, but he doesn't respond or look up at me. I hate that his eyes aren't on me, and I realize the cold from outside has followed us here, only this time the frigidness is flowing from him rather than the north wind sweeping across the property.

"He moved a woman in with him," I continue. "She was a very nice lady, helped me carry my things to my car."

"So, I'm a consolation prize?"

When his eyes meet mine, I can see he's already shutting down. Whatever hope he may have had before is dwindling rapidly.

"I felt absolutely nothing when she opened the door. I wasn't angry or sad or disappointed. I didn't care that my things were packed away, or that she replaced the throw pillows on the sofa and the art on the walls. It didn't bother me that she rearranged the furniture, situating the sofa on the east wall even though it makes no sense because the setting sun glares on the television. None of that mattered. I wasn't upset or sad when Jason showed up and begged me to stay. I didn't feel any of the things I felt when you came home from Venezuela and ignored me. I didn't feel heartbroken about Jason like I do every time you make me feel like an obligation."

His face grows angry, and unlike it would've made me feel weeks ago, I'm no longer scared. I no longer want to back away from him or kiss his lips, so he won't physically hurt me like the men in Miami did. I'm not saying I'd stand as tall as I am right now if it were anyone else, but I know I can trust Ryan, with my safety at least. I have no idea what's about to happen to my heart.

"Not one second since you arrived here have you ever been an obligation," he counters. "I wanted you here every single second."

"Wanted?" I whisper, more to myself than to him.

A word in past tense never hurt me more than that one just did.

"Want," he corrects. "I want you here, but your arrival in my life has complicated things."

"Complicated things?" I want to focus on that, but his back-and-forth is giving me whiplash, so first things first. "What's complicated is you saying all these amazing things to me. Insinuating that you want to be with me as more than a comforting person in my life. You wanted to say things I wasn't ready to hear, which hinted at wanting to move forward in our relationship, and then you get home and won't even make eye contact with me. You let me hold you that night, and then you were gone before the sun came up."

"You distract me," he spits. His face flushes with frustration, but it's gone in a second, and he refocuses on his hands.

I want to yank his head up by twisting my fingers in his hair, but that kind of physical contact would be wrong. Aggression isn't the way for either of us to handle this situation.

"You distract me, too." It's the truth, but his distractions have helped me feel better. I get the distinct impression that the way I'm distracting him isn't resulting in positive outcomes.

"I was so focused on revenge and retribution on your behalf, that I almost got Jinx and myself killed in Venezuela."

My knees go weak, but I'm able to catch myself before I crash to the floor. "What?"

Sad eyes meet mine. "I wanted to tear Jiménez apart piece by piece. I wanted him to beg to live, and then after I spent hours hurting him, I wanted him to beg to die, but I was so focused on what I wanted to do, I missed him pulling a gun. The bruises on my chest were the result of that."

"You were shot!" Tears flood my eyes and fall down my cheeks, and suddenly it's harder to breathe. He had three huge purple bruises on his torso when he got home. That's three chances that evil man had to end his life.

He shrugs. "It happens."

I shake my head, instantly rejecting the thought that they get shot, and it seems to be no big deal to him.

"That's not the problem. The issue is not being able to concentrate because you're clouding my head, compromising my judgement. I can't stop thinking about you, and in a normal man's life that wouldn't be so bad, but mistakes in my line of work can cost me my life or those of the guys on my team. I was stupid in South America, and I can't let it happen again."

My throat works on a rough swallow, the lump forming threatening to keep me from speaking.

"So, I need to leave then?"

Chapter 29

Scooter

I look up at her, and I hate the pain and unwanted acceptance in her eyes.

She nods, but it seems like she's trying to convince herself rather than me.

"I always knew this was a possibility." Her lips attempt a sad smile, but they fail.

Standing from the bed, I walk into the hall and grab the handle to her suitcase before going next door to the room that was hers before.

I know she thinks I'm ending things. That was clear as day on her pretty face, and maybe I'm a little bit of an asshole for letting her continue thinking that for a few minutes, but hell if this woman didn't gut me when she left without warning and then spent two weeks without so much as a peep. I'm hurting her, and that's petty as fuck, but she hurt me, too. She needs to know that my emotions are just as important as hers.

I see silent sobs shaking her shoulders when I turn back to face her, and I want to comfort her. I want to wrap my arms around her and never let her go, but I know that much contact would demolish any restraint I'm trying to manage.

"I'll catch a flight first thing in the morning," she says through her tears. "I should've called instead of coming all the way—"

I press my fingers to her lips to silence her.

"You're not going anywhere, but we need to take things slowly."

Her lips move against my fingers, but I keep her silent by pressing just a little harder. It's not enough to hurt her, and it's not aggressive in any way, but just enough to get my point across.

"We can talk about everything over dinner."

Her eyes narrow as they search mine for answers. I know I've confused her, and I seriously want to explain everything right now, but patience on both our parts will benefit both of us more in the end. Rushing will only lead to problems, and God knows we've had our fair share of those.

Her lips are soft against the calloused tips of my fingers and knowing just how those lips feel against mine makes it hard for me to step back from her. Space is the last thing I want, but I'm ramped up right now. I didn't know she was coming. I had no time to try and wrap my head around her being here again.

She's crying because I'm the biggest asshole in the world, and yet my cock is hard for her, an iron spike in my jeans. I can't control it, but that doesn't mean my mind isn't cataloging all the things I want to do to her, with her, for her.

She needs understanding and reassurance that I'm not going anywhere, I'm not a man who can't get a handle on his own fucking hormones.

The second I pull my finger back, she licks her lips, and even though I don't think she did it on purpose, the tip of her tongue inadvertently touches my finger, and it does absolutely nothing to squelch the situation below my waist. If anything, it makes it ten times worse, to the point that I'm warring with wondering if one little kiss won't hurt.

Only I know it wouldn't stop there. A peck on the lips would turn into the brush of my tongue on her plump lower lip. She'd gasp, and I'd be forced to seek her own tongue. She'd release a breathy moan, and then what little restraint I had would fly out the damn window. My hands would be on her, seeking to explore all the areas I've only been able to imagine up to this point. Next her—

No. Stop.

I shake my head as my fingers itch to readjust my erection, but I don't want to draw anymore attention to the damn thing.

"Dinner?" she asks innocently, her eyes still on mine. She's unaware of my struggle right now, and I want to keep it that way.

No pressure and taking things slow also means finding some way to keep my damn self under control. I need her setting the pace, and since my cock is yelling *full steam ahead*, I know I can't trust myself to drive this situation.

"You cook?" she continues when I can't focus enough to speak.

I chuckle, a throaty sound that is really misplaced right now but she doesn't seem to notice.

"I don't cook." I clear my throat when the words come out husky and seductive rather than informative as I'd attempted. "We're going out to eat."

I expect her to shut down, for apprehension to fill her pretty brown eyes, but instead of backing away from me and holding up her hands to reject the offer, she smiles, a bright perfect sight I've only seen a couple of times up to this point.

"Is that okay?" I ask, hoping I'm not misjudging her reaction.

"Dinner sounds perfect."

Her eyes are still rimmed in red from crying, and her cheeks are wet from tears that have stopped falling, but she's still the most beautiful woman I've ever laid eyes on. She's pretty in her brokenness, but Lord give me strength if she isn't absolutely divine in her healing.

"I need to shower and get ready. Is an hour long enough for you to do the same?"

"That's plenty of time," she assures me.

I give her a curt nod before turning back to leave the room, but her arm reaches out, clasping onto my bicep to prevent me from walking away.

"Ryan?"

A rush of air leaves my lungs at the breathy way my name leaves her lips.

"Yeah?"

She doesn't say a word as she steps in front of me and wraps her arms around my waist. She smells like the perfect combination of every single thing that's good in the world. She's happiness and serenity, Christmas and spring. I breathe her in, unable to resist planting my nose against the top of her head.

I could do this for hours, just standing here with my arms around her, but she doesn't linger, and the hug is over too soon. She gives me a shy smile as she steps back, and I take it as my chance to leave. Getting my thoughts, hormones, and expectations under control may take longer than the hour of time I've allotted before dinner, but I'll do my best.

The shame I've always felt when I stroked off to thoughts of her before don't hit me this time around. The softness of her skin. The way her eyelashes brush her cheeks like butterfly wings when she's tired but fighting sleep. The warmth of her breath against my skin the last night she was here. All of it filters in while the regret, discomfort, and derision never show.

Things are different. She's different than she was a few weeks ago, and excitement warms my blood as I get dressed. Maybe the break was exactly what she needed?

I stay in my room until ten minutes before we're to leave, but anxiousness draws me out. A quick peek tells me that her door is closed, so I make my way to the living room, praying I don't walk in on something crazy going on between Max and Jasmine. I'm all for sexual freedom but seeing my boss's daughter naked and in a compromising position isn't an image I want in my head.

I don't have to worry about a damn thing because Mia is already in the living room when I round the corner. I want to kick myself for wasting time in my bedroom, but her smile smooths everything over.

"Where are you two going?" Max asks as I step closer.

"Mind your business," Mia tells him, but there's laughter in her voice, and it makes me wonder what they were discussing before I showed up.

Mia stands, walking to me in a way that makes what I did in the shower irrelevant. All the bruises on her face are gone, and even though her arm is still in a cast, she looks perfectly healthy.

"You're gorgeous," I whisper when she steps closer.

Her clothes must be ones she got from home, because she's in jeans and a nice top, rather than leggings and one of my old t-shirts, which she arrived in earlier.

Her fingers toy with the space left open from the top button of my shirt being undone.

"Ready to go?"

She smiles up at me in answer, and I can't help but imagine how tonight is going to go.

Chapter 30

Mia

Has he always been this handsome, or have I been blind to his appeal?

Well, not completely blind, of course. There isn't a single unattractive man in Cerberus that I've seen. Every one of them are in the prime of their lives, physically fit, and an air about them that makes women stop and take a look, but Ryan is the epitome of handsome. Add in his ability to be patient, kind, and protective, and he's the perfect man. How did I ever get on a plane and walk away from him?

The softness of his hair makes me want to run my fingers through it, but he's also trimmed his beard, leaving behind a hint of scruff, and that's beyond appealing as well.

"I'm ready," I tell him, agreeing once again to dinner, but my voice is husky, and from the way his eyes widen and his throat works, I can tell he's feeling the same attraction that I am.

He helps me into my coat as Jasmine and Max watch our interaction. My brother's attention was split between the game on the TV and Jasmine, but now, Ryan and I are garnering all of his attention. I'm in a better position now to discuss Max's history, death, and reappearance, but Ryan is my only concern right now.

I hate the thickness of my coat as Ryan places his palm to my back and guides me toward the door. I want to feel the heat of his touch, but there will be time for that later. I hope.

Like a gentleman and unlike Jason's behavior, he opens the passenger door of an SUV and waits for me to climb inside and get my seatbelt on before he closes the door. After climbing inside, he cranks the car, turning the heater up full blast, and we grin at each other as we fist our hands near our mouths and blow air on them to warm our fingers.

"I can't get over how cold it is here," I mumble around my hands.

"Nebraska is much colder," he says. "At least there isn't snow right now. I hate driving in that shit."

We make small talk all the way into town. He urges me to wait for him as he climbs out of the SUV outside of the diner, and I'm grinning like a fool when he opens the passenger door for me and offers a hand to take as I climb out.

"Thank you," I whisper, realizing how far manners go, especially after everything that's happened to me.

A waitress seats us quickly in a booth in the back and takes our drink order before walking away. Instead of sitting across from me, Ryan positions himself beside me, so we can both see the entire dining area. I pull a napkin from the dispenser and begin to shred it, but unlike while I was meeting with Jason, I'm not filled with doubt, worry, and abundant frustrations. I am nervous. He said we'll have our serious discussion at dinner, and I don't know if he's bringing me to a public place to tell me things are over or if he needs people around so he can keep things slow like he mentioned back at the clubhouse.

I don't think it's the former, but I've learned to stop making assumptions.

"Listen I—"

"What I—"

We begin at the same time. We both pause to laugh, and even though he's a gentleman, he begins again instead of deferring to me to speak my mind.

"What I wanted to talk about is serious." He looks around at the smiling people enjoying their meals. "I don't know if this is the best place."

"Nope." I shake my head and turn slightly in my seat so I can see his face better. "You're not getting out of this that easily, but if it makes you feel better, I can go first."

His eyes search mine as if he's trying to determine what I have to say. I wasn't very nice to him back in his room, and even though I had wanted to say exactly what I did, I also didn't want to resort to getting angry and pointing blame.

He nods eventually, but I pause before speaking, noticing our waitress returning to the table with our drinks and a basket of warm, fresh rolls.

The wait for our discussion is even longer because resisting the carbs on the table is impossible for me. I've eaten what I needed since getting rescued, but after my conversation with Jason and my middle-of-the-night epiphany at my parents, I've been ravenous. It's like I'm making up for the calorie deficiency from the last couple of months.

"Good?" Ryan asks with a grin as I devour half the roll in one bite.

My mouth is stuffed full so all I can do is nod.

"So good," I tell him after I swallow. "Get one."

"Maybe later," he says as his eyebrows go up, indicating that he's waiting for me to speak.

"I shouldn't have left the way I did. I'm not going to apologize for going because it was exactly what I needed, but not letting you know I was going back home was rude." I place the remaining half of my roll on the small plate and wipe my fingers on a napkin. He deserves all of my attention no matter how much I really want to eat the entire basket of bread. "I did a lot of thinking while I was away. I cleaned a lot of things off my plate."

His lip twitches, and I wonder if he's aware, due to my response to the bread, just how much I've been eating.

I clear my throat to hide my smile. I'm trying to be serious, and he's distracting me from saying what needs to be said.

"I don't see you as just the guy who rescued me. When I look into your eyes, I can picture a future with you. I like the idea of slow, but at the same time I feel like we've been crawling at a snail's pace. You've been there for me, comforted me, kept me safe from the demons when they tried to sneak in. You've been my sounding board, and my champion when I wasn't strong enough to fight for myself. You stood up to my brother in Miami and wouldn't take no for an answer when I wanted to come back with you to New Mexico even though I'd only known you for a couple of days."

I bite me lip to force myself to pause because my words are rushing out, and I'm saying too much too fast and I don't want to lose him or cheapen the moment.

"You've held me in your arms while ignoring your own body. You haven't pushed me to take things further, and I know how hard that can be for a man, but you're not controlled by desire and lust. You never once made me feel like you expected something of me when I asked you to give me things daily. I need the warmth of your body and your arms around me to feel safe. I needed your company, your stories, and when it was too much, I also needed some space. You gave that all to me without question. But you also followed me with your eyes. You'd watch me the way a man watches a woman he's interested in, not like a man guarding someone he feels he has to protect."

"I didn't mean to look at you that way," he interrupts, and my face falls.

Refusing to leave this diner confused or unsure of where we stand, I rush out, "Because you don't see me that way or—"

His eyes sparkle. "No, I definitely see you that way, but I didn't mean for that to show so soon."

I cup his jaw with my hand, finally getting the chance to feel the rough stubble on his cheeks. "I want you to look at me that way, and even though I wasn't ready to see you as more than a protector then, I am now."

"Spell it out for me, Sweet Mia," he begs.

"I want you in that way. I really like you, and I'm insanely attracted to you."

"I missed you like crazy when you were gone. I was on the verge of going mad."

"I handled it poorly," I confess. "It won't happen again."

"It can't." He swallows again. "If we're going to do this. If we're going to be more than friends, I need to know where we stand at all times. I've already been suspended for a month."

"Suspended?" I don't mean to interrupt him, but he's been dealing with more than I was even aware.

"Mistakes were made in South America," he reminds me.

Like I could ever forget.

"There are consequences, and if they let me go back out in the field, I have to have my head on straight. I won't ever stop worrying about you. It's not ever going to be possible, but I need to be able to do my job without distractions. At least while I'm physically working."

"If you want me to stay, I'm here. I love my parents, but I can't ever see New Orleans being my home. There's too much darkness, too many things tainting it for me. I know I was being presumptuous coming back here, but I don't want you to say things or promise things you aren't a hundred percent sure of."

He nods, looking relieved when the waitress returns to take our orders. The last time she stopped by, we hadn't even looked at our menus. Right now is no different, but instead of asking her to come back again, Ryan orders for both of us. He must be aware of my current carb obsession because he orders me French toast with eggs and hash browns.

I hate the interruption because I feel like it derailed us, but then Ryan turns in his seat and clasps my hands, picking up right where we left off a few moments ago.

"I know I want you in my life. I know I want you in my bed." His eyes dart between mine, and I wonder if he's wanting to say something that he feels like I'm not ready to hear. He said as much during our conversation while he was out of the country.

"Don't hide the truth or your feelings from me," I beg.

"I want everything you have to offer, and probably things you won't be ready to give for a long time, if ever, but I want you to know I'm a patient man. Holding you, being near you soothes something in my soul I didn't know needed soothing. But at the same time, I want your lips on mine. I want my mouth on every inch of your body. I want to remind you that physical pleasure is a good thing, but I don't want to do anything until you're ready. We're taking this at your pace, and I wouldn't be able to live with myself if you feel obligated or you do something you'll regret later. Just know that my cock is going to get hard, and I'm going to watch you like I can't take my eyes off you, because I can't."

"I dated Jason for eight years. For almost a decade, I spent nearly every day with the same man," I tell him. "What I felt for him, what I thought I felt for him doesn't even begin to compare to what I feel for you. I'm not going to use the L word right now because I don't want to leap too soon, but this isn't temporary for me. I'm not going to wake up tomorrow and change my mind. I need to know that you aren't either."

His face softens as his grip on my hands grows. "Sweet Mia, I'm in this for the long haul."

Chapter 31

Scooter

We talked at the diner for hours. After we got the heavy stuff out of the way, Mia shared bits and pieces of her past with me. She was guarded in some areas. She still doesn't want to talk about her abduction or her time spent there, but I get the feeling that those things are easier discussed in the darkness where she can feel my warmth against her body for comfort.

When the waitress finally had enough of us taking up the table in her section, making it clear we should leave by removing our empty drink cups from the table rather than offering us another refill, we left.

I know we talked about not wondering where things were going or where we stand, but I delay getting her back to the clubhouse because I also insisted that we take things slow. I don't know if our confessions over French toast and eggs trumps that insistence or if it's still in place.

"We do a lot of community work around here," I tell her as we drive through town. "We host cookouts at the park. We've taken our bikes to the fire department while they're having canned food drives, so it draws more people in who want to get pictures. Cerberus organizes blood drives, and at least three times a year we do poker runs, and around Christmas we do a toy run as well."

"So, nothing like Sons of Anarchy?"

I snort a laugh. I know there are clubs out there that are hedonistic to their core. Ravens Ruin in Massachusetts comes to mind, but Cerberus isn't like that at all. From inception, the club has been about helping and giving back. Hell, it's part of the mission statement posted on the wall in the living room.

"The parties can get a little wild sometimes," I tell her. "The guys like to blow off steam when they get home."

"The guys?" She smiles at me with her eyebrows raised. "Not you?"

"Things are different now."

I focus on driving, hoping she'll drop it, but once Mia starts chatting it's hard to get her to stop.

"You don't have to change things like that for me. I'm not telling you that I'm going to be right in the middle of it, but I don't want you to feel like you can't do what you'd normally do just because we're together."

Together. Never before have three syllables sounded so damn good.

I clear my throat, wondering if I should tell her the full truth, and then I remind myself that she said not to hide from her. "Drinking beer and getting rowdy with the guys isn't what I imagine doing when I get home from a mission."

I can feel her eyes on the side of my face as I turn on the road leading to the clubhouse, and I know she isn't going to let me off the hook that easily.

"If I've been away from you for any length of time, you're who I'd want to spend time with. I'm not going to want beer or loud music, I'm going to want—"

My jaw snaps shut. Mentally, I feel like we're on the same page, but Mia is miles away from being ready for the intimate stuff and talking about it may only lead to her feeling that obligation I insisted she shouldn't feel.

"What?" she prods. "What would you want?"

"Your touch. Your arms around me. I'll want to look into your pretty eyes and be reminded why we continue to do what we do even though it's dangerous."

"I want that, too," she whispers, and my heart is filled to the top and overflowing with all the good things life has to give by the time we pull up outside of the clubhouse.

I don't want the night to end, so I don't turn the SUV off after putting it into park. I wasn't joking when I told her I wanted to spend all my time with her. Tonight is no different. The last two weeks of her being gone was just as bad as it would've been if I were the one gone.

"Has Jasmine been staying here with Max while Kingston is gone?" Mia asks, her eyes focused on the front of the clubhouse.

"Most nights. Max is working for Cerberus now, so he sticks pretty close in case they need something from him."

"He seems happy," she whispers. "With both of them. He and Kingston were best friends growing up, and when that friendship morphed into something else the dedication was a tangible thing between the two of them. I envied them. I wanted that for myself, but then Kingston walked away from Max, and the devastation my brother felt was horrendous." She sighs. "I think watching that made me leery of getting too serious, but it also made me complacent. It made me stay with Jason because I was afraid of how I'd feel without him. I was afraid of making a mistake."

I take her hand, but she still looks off in the distance as if she can see more than just fields covered in darkness.

"I don't think being here is a mistake, and if that means that my abduction had to happen for this series of events to play, for me to be right here with you in this moment, then that may not be a mistake either. And that scares the shit out of me. Does it make me crazy?"

She finally turns her head, and I hate the tears clinging to her lower lashes.

"No. Not at all. I'm a firm believer that everything happens for a reason. The good, the bad, the tragic. The sequence of events in our lives happen when they're supposed to. I think it's a very enlightened way of thinking for you to be able to accept that."

She chuckles. "Really?"

I shrug. "Kincaid made me see a shrink for an evaluation after Venezuela. Dr. Alverez said some things that made a lot of sense. I've had a couple appointments with her the last two weeks, and she's helping me work through my own shit."

"I think Camryn mentioned her to me once. I may have to take her suggestion and make an appointment myself."

I squeeze her hand one more time before releasing it to turn the SUV off. "I think that's an amazing idea. Let's get inside. I know you have to be tired after traveling all day."

The clubhouse is silent when we walk inside, so I make sure to lock the door behind us. I'm dragging my feet toward the hallway, and I can tell Mia is, too. Neither one of us want to say goodnight, but I stop outside of her door, anyway.

"Thank you for dinner," she says as she turns to face me.

"Anytime. I'm glad we got a lot of things settled."

Like ripping off a Band-Aid and trying to get this over with so I can go to my room and question myself on the million other ways I wish this night would go, I lean down and press my mouth to hers. I'm planning a nice, quick kiss, something that will leave me wanting more than I already do, but Mia has other plans. Her fingers tangle in the front of my shirt as she lifts up onto the tips of her toes to deepen it.

It's my turn to gasp, allowing her seeking tongue entrance to my mouth. Just like I imagined earlier. She still releases that tiny moan, though. Pulling her against me, I angle my head. Jesus, she feels amazing against me, and I'd love nothing more than to lift her feet from the ground and carry her to my room. I still have two weeks of suspension left, and I can think of a few dozen things we could do to fill the time.

But then she pulls away, blinking up at me like something has changed right before her eyes.

"Sleep well, Sweet Mia," I whisper, brushing my lips across her cheek because I just have to touch her one more time.

"You, too," she pants, and I have to walk away before I make myself a liar. Yes, I'm a patient man, but she's a temptation I can barely resist.

Her bedroom door clicks closed just as I enter my own room. I'm exhausted, the weight of being without her the last two weeks has lifted, reminding me just how little sleep I've gotten while she was away, but I also know that I'll drive myself mad by morning time with her being so close and still just out of reach.

Stripping down to my boxer briefs, I climb between the cool sheets and sigh. My eyes focus on the wall that separates our rooms, but eventually my eyes flutter closed. Dreaming about her is a much better option than lying here awake and pining for her.

The clock on my bedside table reads two am when my bedroom door creaks open.

When Mia steps inside of my room, I'm well aware that I need to ask her to leave. My strength only goes so far, and her confessions and deciding that we want to be together has used up every ounce of my reserves.

I don't ask her to leave. I knew that if I did, I'd just end up following her to her room to admit my mistake.

Chapter 32

Mia

I ignore the voice in my head that's telling me to turn back around and leave his room. That voice has done me wrong so many times over the last couple of weeks, and I'm learning to ignore it. At least, I'm doing my best. The whispers in my head are lying. He does want to spend time with me. He does want the same things I do. He doesn't despise me. He doesn't wish I'd stayed in Louisiana nor does he wish he'd never met me.

So, I ignore the self-esteem issues I've been struggling with and walk closer to his bed. He knows I'm here. He's too much of a soldier to let anyone sneak up on him. His body tensed when the tiny stream of light from the hallway hit the end of his bed, but he remains silent.

Then I see him looking up at me, and even though I'm ignoring those voices in my head, I don't miss the expression on his face that's telling me without a doubt that he's torn between welcoming me into his arms and asking me to leave.

He doesn't want me to leave because he doesn't want me here. He's afraid that I'll do something I'll regret later, and he never wants me to feel regret where he's concerned. He said as much during dinner tonight.

I open my mouth to tell him that I feel like a fool, but when I give that thought a breath of life, I realize that I don't feel that way at all. I'm not in here because I'm scared to sleep alone. I'm here, standing in his room, because I want to be next to him. He thinks I want slow, but he has to realize that we've been doing slow for weeks and weeks. My presence in his room isn't moving fast. It isn't taking things too far too soon. This is the right speed. The perfect speed.

Even though we spent the last two weeks apart, I spent most of that time not only evaluating my past but also thinking of my future, and Ryan is a huge part of that. I want to be in his arms, in his bed, with him inside of me. Before I even left my parents' house, I knew I wanted him. It didn't take seeing him again, and although the conversation we had at the diner helped, it was needed for me to know that I'd fight for him if that's what it took.

Yet, a fight isn't needed. He wants me as much as I want him, and that's the scary part. This feels almost too easy. Things haven't been easy for a long time. I understand complicated. I understand difficult situations.

Effortless is new to me.

"Come here," he whispers, his voice a soft plea.

I want to do exactly that, but my feet feel cemented to the floor. This room, the way he's looking up at me is exactly the way it's been dozens of times since I first came to New Mexico. The clouds of all of those other times circle around me like a thunderstorm ready to unleash havoc and pain. He's held me in his arms in here countless times. I spent hours sobbing into his chest before draining every ounce of energy I had. I clung to him when I felt empty and broken, and even though I know what I want now, even though I feel like things are looking up, no matter the level of bravado I try to convince myself I have, I'm still broken. I'm still in a million tiny pieces, only now I have hope that I won't stay that way.

Ryan has the ability to put me back together, and he's been doing just that since the first time my swollen eyes met his in that Miami compound.

"Mia?" He shifts his weight, lifting up on his elbows as he waits for me to make my decision. When I don't respond immediately, he turns on the bedside table lamp. I both love and hate the light now shining between us. Confessions are easier made in the dark, but at the same time I don't want anything misconstrued between us.

"I feel ashamed," I confess as he watches me patiently.

"You don't have to," he assures me. "No one is judging you for being afraid."

My throat works on a swallow. "I'm not afraid. Fear of being in my own room isn't what drew me in here."

"Talk to me."

Sitting up on the side of his bed, he reaches for my hand, and I let him take it. He doesn't pull me closer. He's merely offering me a lifeline, a human touch to ease the war inside of my head. He's been the only one whose touch soothed me in a way I can't describe. He brings peace, tranquility, and ease to the scattered thoughts in my head. Just the brush of his fingertips does what the sedatives were meant to do in the hospital.

"I want you."

He smiles up at me, the right side of his mouth twitching in that way that I love, but he doesn't tell me that he feels the same.

"I need you."

"I'm here." He releases my hand, opening his arms, and I don't waste a second stepping into his embrace, but a hug isn't what I'm after.

Instead of pulling him to my chest, I straddle his thighs. A rush of air escapes his perfect lips when my center brushes him.

"Mia?" It's a plea, a whimper begging for mercy.

"Is it wrong that I want you after everything that's happened?"

He bites his lip when I circle my hips. He's hard, a thick stalk between my legs, and my body sings with the contact. I shudder, feeling the full force of arousal for the first time in as long as I can remember, but this isn't only about me. I know that at least his body wants this, too, but his body always responds to mine. This doesn't mean that his head is in the same place.

"Jesus," he grips my hips, but he isn't trying to hold me in place.

He doesn't stop me, but I need the words. I need to know that I'm not forcing his hand. He has to be an active participant in this as well. The worry of regret goes two ways, and the last thing I want is for him to feel forced. God, I'd never want someone to feel compelled to go along with something they really didn't want.

"Do you want this?" My body shivers when I stop moving, but I don't want him to make decisions based on his own body's need. I need his head fully engaged.

His head tilts back, his eyes focusing first on my mouth before they reach my eyes.

"Only if it's what you want," he whispers.

"I do." I bite my lip to keep from moaning when he shifts his weight. The thin layers of clothing between us aren't doing much to impede the sensations.

"We can stop at any point. If you change your min—"

I silence him up with a kiss, pressing my lips to his and wasting no time letting my tongue brush against his. His fingers tighten on my hips, and he groans in my mouth. The sound reverberates through my body and settles right where I need him the most.

"Ryan," I pant when we come up for air.

"Tell me I'm not dreaming," he says, his lips brushing down my neck as his fingers find the skin between my sleep shorts and t-shirt. "Tell me this isn't another one my fantasies, and that I'm not going to wake up without you."

My lips twitch as I lean back enough to look at his face. "You fantasize about me?"

He nods as his cheeks pink. I brush my fingertips against his face. "I can't control my dreams, but I do it more than I should while I'm awake."

"Tell me about them," I urge.

I want to give him exactly what he wants, but he isn't falling for it. "Tonight is about you. Want you want. What you need."

"I want you to enjoy this, too."

A wicked smile crosses his face as his tongue snakes out to lick his lower lip. "Oh, Sweet Mia. I'm going to enjoy every minute of it."

This is a plan I can get behind. "Touch me."

His hands leave my hips, but he doesn't toss me on the bed and take over. His fingers press against my back until I lean closer, a gasp leaving my lips when he wraps his mouth over my nipple through the cotton of my shirt. Wet heat blooms against my breast and between my legs.

Not wanting to waste another minute, I tug my shirt over my head and toss it to the floor. He doesn't attack my breasts like I expect. His eyes focus on my chest, and he seems torn with which dark-tipped breast he should focus on.

"Jesus, Mia," he murmurs. "You're fucking perfect."

I make the decision for him, angling my body so the furled point of my left breast presses against his lips. He moans like a man starved as he sucks the sensitive flesh into his mouth. Chills and desire race down my spine, and I let myself get lost in the sensations I didn't think I'd ever feel again.

Any shame I was feeling about wanting this after everything that has happened fades away. The guilt and sorrow are no longer in the room. It's only him and I and our desperate need for each other, and what a relief that is.

He devours my flesh, licking and nipping and moving his head between the two globes like he's afraid one will get jealous of the other. He grows impossibly bigger between my thighs and becomes increasingly harder to ignore.

Who am I to receive such pleasure and not return the favor?

My hands wander down the rippling plains of his chest and abdomen, and I celebrate the ability to touch him with more than comfort in mind. Arching his back to put distance between our torsos without taking his mouth off my skin, he gives me all the permission I need to let my hands roam lower.

He's virile, ready, and hard as stone, the tip of him glistening when I pull the elastic of his boxer briefs away from his body.

Whimpering with need when I stroke my finger over his wetness, Ryan buries his face between my breasts.

Not wanting to lose contact with him, I stand, keeping my feet against his thighs. How I'm cognizant enough to keep my head lowered so I don't get smacked in the head with the fan is beyond me, but I manage. I shove my sleep shorts down along with my panties, but before I can lower myself, Ryan takes advantage and nips at my naked hip. I didn't stand above him to end up like this, but I also don't shy away when he swipes his tongue up the center of me.

"Oh, God," I moan when his tongue explores, splitting me open and attacking the bundle of nerves at the apex of my thighs.

He's ravenous, his talented mouth quickly bringing me to the brink of an orgasm that's sure to leave me spent and useless.

"Ryan," I hiss when my knees grow weak.

He must sense my instability because he wraps his arms around my thighs. His mouth never stops working me over, and I have to clutch his shoulders, rounding my back and leaning over him to keep from falling.

A long-suffered moan rumbles from his chest when I start to convulse against his mouth, and it echoes in my core like a delicious treat that feeds my orgasm, strengthening it until it threatens my vision.

"So perfect," he praises as he guides me back down to straddle his lap.

He doesn't line himself up like I'd hoped, and when I finally regain some of my composure, he's looking at me with so many emotions on his handsome face that it's impossible to sort them out.

"Thank you," I tell him with a soft smile.

"The pleasure was all mine." His fingers brush my cheek, and I can't help but lean into the touch.

He's huge and covered in tattoos. He's scary to anyone who doesn't know him, a force to be reckoned with, yet his touches are feather light and amazing.

I press my lips to his, tasting myself on his mouth as I shove the elastic of his boxers down his hips. Without pulling our mouths apart, he lifts his hips so the fabric can fall free of his legs. He moans when I wrap my fingers around him, but his tongue commands my mouth the exact same way he controlled my body while I was standing.

All it takes is a simple shift of my hips to position him at my entrance, and as much as I want to sink down on him and take him inside of me to the hilt, I need one last assurance from him, so I pull my mouth from his and look down into his half-lidded eyes.

He doesn't give permission with words, he simply grips my hips and urges me down on him. We don't break eye contact as my body takes his cock inside of me. My mouth forms an O from the shear pleasure of feeling him stretch me, and as his eyes flutter closed, I know he's enjoying it as much as I am.

"Mia," he hisses when I settle on his thighs with him fully inside of me.

I'm so wet from the arousal I've felt since I climbed out the cab hours ago and my recent orgasm that the glide is smooth and perfect. In fact, I've never felt such perfection, such unadulterated pleasure before in my life.

"You have to move, baby. God, you feel so fucking good."

When he leans forward to take my mouth, I do exactly what we both need. I use my legs and lift my weight before letting myself fall right back down. I do it over and over and over, building a frenzy between us that's going to leave us both unable to move, breathe, or speak.

With his mouth still on mine, Ryan grips my ass and helps when my legs begin to tremble.

"God, baby, you're getting tighter," he groans into my mouth. "So, fucking tight."

He nips at my lower lip before arching so he can take my nipple in his mouth, and it's over. My body detonates, the orgasm starting in my core and radiating to every other inch of my body. My rhythm stutters, and I feel every muscle in his body tense as he takes over, holding all of my weight and maintaining the rhythm until my release wanes.

"Hold on," he tells me, and I manage enough before he flips us over.

He settles back between my legs, lowering his entire body until he blankets me. I expect him to pound into me, to chase after his own orgasm since it's his turn, but his hips roll slowly with expert precision. His thrusts are measured and hit me exactly where I need him, and before long another orgasm threatens.

"Ryan," I pant, unsure if my body can handle another release.

"Come for me," he whispers against my mouth. "I want to wring every ounce of pleasure from your amazing body."

"Ryan," is all I can mange when he repositions, and his cock strikes that perfect spot inside of me. The relentless stimulation forces me over the edge, but this time when I contract around him, he swells impossibly bigger inside of me and his own rhythmic convulsions mirror my own.

My heart pounds and my breathing mimics a winded runner after a marathon, and my body feels used in the best ways possible.

Chapter 33

Scooter

I have died and gone to heaven. If it weren't for the scrape of Mia's fingernails down my back as her arms fall helplessly to the mattress, I'd think I was dreaming. Sheer perfection doesn't even begin to describe what just happened.

I let her take control, and she did it magnificently. Just the brush of her clothed body against my hard dick was nearly enough to bring me over the edge. It had been so long, so many nights of feeling her against me when there was nothing I could do about it. The days spent in silence, the ones where she wouldn't make a peep unless it was to cry or whimper when she was scared, were different. My head didn't conjure up anything sexual, but eventually she began to talk and let me in. Her soft voice and those infrequent smiles were hell on my body, but I endured, and her gift just now was more than I could've ever hoped for. The bliss was never-ending and utterly splendid.

But the during, the thrill of being inside of her isn't what concerns me. She enjoyed herself, coming three times before we were done, but the after has always been my fear. The regret she legitimately didn't think she would feel.

I remain silent, letting her work through her own thoughts as I lie down beside her and pull her to my chest. If she wants to distance herself from me, she's going to have to work for it.

It doesn't take long before my worst fears come to fruition. Quietly, Mia pulls away from me before climbing off the bed. The click of the bathroom door is like a bomb going off in the middle of a cave. It rattles around in my head as it echoes around the room.

My heart doesn't have the chance to settle down. It ramps up again. Only this time it isn't racing as a side effect of the most amazing sex I've ever had in my life. It's pounding against my ribcage in fear. That trepidation makes me bolt off the bed and rush to the bathroom door, but before I can lift my hand to knock, the door swings open.

Mia looks up at me sheepishly.

"Mia, I—"

"You came inside of me," she whispers, her cheeks a bright pink.

"I did," I confirm, gallons if I go by the number of times my cock jerked inside of her.

"It's messy." A shy smile plays across her pretty face, and I realize I read the entire situation wrong.

I bite the inside of my cheek as I look down at her. I don't bring up the obvious consequences of what we did, and neither does she. We both know what could happen, but I don't think she's ready for me to tell her that the sight of watching her belly grow with my child is something I'm eventually going to want.

Just imagining how heavy her tits would be, filled with the nourishment for our child, makes me groan and my cock begins to thicken again.

"Do you hate messy?" I ask, a half-assed attempt at distracting my dick.

"I don't want to sleep in a wet spot," she says, and her eyes grow bright and full of the same emotion I saw on her pretty face when she first climbed out of the cab earlier.

Unable to go a second longer without knowing for sure, I curl my finger under her chin so I can fully look in her eyes. "Are we okay?"

"I'm perfect," she answers. "It was amazing."

She slides past me to climb back in the bed, and I take the opportunity to piss and wash up a little before joining her under the covers.

Amazing.

My sentiments exactly. Being with her was phenomenal, better than I could've ever imagined.

I don't waste a second pulling her to my chest when I climb back in the bed. She didn't bother with clothes, so neither do I.

My body still yearns for her, my cock taking notice of her naked flesh against my own, but I ignore it. I know one time won't be enough, but the ball is in her court, and it will be so long as I even think there's a chance she isn't ready for all I have to offer. My needs are secondary to hers, and they always will be. I want to shower her with every affection I was never able to show any woman prior to her.

She releases a breathy sigh of contentment, the warmth skating over my chest, and I hold her tighter.

"No regrets?" I ask because I'm dying to know. She isn't showing any outward signs of being upset over what we did, but I have to make sure.

"None whatsoever," she says, and I feel her lips pull into a smile.

My heart is absolutely full, brimming to the top and overflowing. It should make me feel like a pussy, like a silly sap for being content with holding her, but those emotions don't even touch me.

"No guilt?"

She's not as quick to respond this time, and the silence says more than words ever could.

I press my lips to the top of her head. "Please, never feel guilty for doing what you want, for taking pleasure, for enjoying something that was once used against you as a weapon."

Her hot tears roll down my side, and as much as I want to lift her off me to stare in her eyes and repeat those words until she believes them, I just hold her even tighter.

"You may have to remind of this sometimes."

"Every day for the rest of your life," I vow. "You're precious, Mia. A gift I've always needed and never thought to ask for."

"I could say the same about you."

My hand works up her spine and back down again, the action familiar and soothing to both of us. Tonight was a big step, and one I hope happens again very soon, but I'd be a fool to think that she's healed completely. There will be setbacks and days when she can't see past the grief and anger. Days when it'll take everything I have to keep reminding her that she's amazing and perfect, not in spite of what happened to her but because it did.

Not many women could come out the other side with hopes and dreams and goals to work toward, but I have this feeling deep inside of me that Mia Vazquez is going to surprise every single one of us. Her abduction might have broken her, but she's still a force that will overcome and conquer. Hell, she's already turned my rugged ass into a love-sick fool, a man dependent on her touch.

"I hope my brother and Jasmine didn't hear what we did."

Max's room is on one side of mine and Mia's on the other. A wicked grin crosses my lips.

"It would only be payback," I mutter. "You wouldn't believe the shit I've had to listen to the last couple of weeks."

She huffs a laugh against my chest.

"I never knew how fucking bossy Tug was until a few nights ago. He commanded them like a general even while being in South America."

"South America?"

"That's where the guys are right now, but you'd think he was in the same room with them rather than thousands of miles away. His voice echoes through the walls as he got very specific on what you're damn brother needed to do to their woman."

I won't tell her that it turned me on. I still feel a little guilty for lying in bed and taking care of how my body responded to the way Tug told Max *exactly* how Jasmine's pussy should be treated.

And now I'm getting hard again. Damn it.

"Doesn't surprise me," Mia whispers. "They were so loud when they were in high school. My headphones were practically glued to my ears to try and drown out their noises."

"Well, turnabouts fair play I guess."

"I need to talk to him." I know she's talking about Max.

Her brother has tried numerous times to comfort her, but I think she's holding onto a grudge for him faking his own death all those years ago. It would hurt anyone, but after what she went through, I think it hit her even harder.

"I think he's ready for that conversation," I tell her.

I tilt her chin up and press my lips to hers, but it isn't a prequel to anything but a goodnight.

"Sleep, Sweet Mia. It's been a long day."

She grins against my lips before dropping her head back to my chest and sinking down further on the mattress.

Yep, this is heaven.

Chapter 34

Mia

Before I even open my eyes, I know Ryan is gone.

The same fear that engulfed me after he left me alone when they got back from Venezuela threatens to rear its ugly head again, but I shove it down and take stock of my surroundings.

His leather cut, the one he never leaves the clubhouse without is still tossed over the back of the chair in the corner. His boots are to the side of the TV stand, and the sound of water can be heard from the bathroom.

He hasn't left at all, and I feel foolish for thinking he would after last night.

Even though he isn't gone, I still question whether or not I should join him in the shower, but my body begs for warm water and a good scrubbing. I cleaned up as best I could last night, but the pull of him was stronger than the urge to bathe and it finally forced me out of the bathroom and into his arms.

Telling myself to get out of my head, I climb out of the bed and go to him. At first sight, I think something is wrong. His head is dropped low as the water shoots between his shoulder blades, and I immediately realize how easy it is to see him through the opaque shower curtain. We spent the better part of a week with him standing guard, with his back turned, while I showered. At any given second he could've looked over his shoulder and gotten an eye full, but even though I didn't always focus on him to make sure he kept his distance, I know deep in my soul that he never once tried to get a glimpse of me before I was willing to give it to him.

Ryan Gabhart is an honorable man, and I'm not fool enough to let him go anytime soon.

"You just going to gawk at me, or are you going to join me?"

His rough voice snaps me out of my thoughts, and I give him a smile. I should feel out of place standing naked in his bathroom with his eyes drilling holes in me, but I don't. My feet move, carrying me to him. He holds the curtain open, uncaring that water is dripping from his arm to the floor as I climb inside. Cold droplets and mist from the water hitting his body force a wave of chills over my skin, and I know without looking down that my nipples have turned into tight buds. They don't miss his attention either, but he doesn't let his eyes linger.

There's a dirtiness in his gaze, but it's nothing like the men who hurt me before. There's not one single thing about this man that is reminiscent of those evil people. That salacious look in his eyes makes my body thrum with anticipation not the urge to cower away and protect myself.

I step closer to him until his thickening erection hits my stomach. With my eyes on his face, the brush of it on my abdomen startles me.

"Ignore it," he commands in a husky voice.

I bite the inside of my lip before a coy smile can take over my face.

I've never been a wanton, needy woman before. I've never wanted to spend countless hours in bed, completely wrapped around a man. Sure, Jason and I spent a lot of time vegging out, but boredom was quick to settle in. I get the feeling that Ryan and I can spend the next twelve months in his room only leaving for food, and it still wouldn't be long enough to satiate myself with his body.

"Ignore it?" I ask, my eyes still on his.

It takes all my willpower not to look down at the part of him that was inside of me last night. I felt every thick inch, but never really got a good look at it. I was afraid seeing it would make me think it was a weapon exactly like he spoke of last night before letting me fall asleep in his arms.

"Yeah."

"Is that what you really want?" My eyes rake down his body. He is absolutely magnificent, his body a work of art and a well-trained machine. In the full light of the bathroom, I take my time letting my fingers trace every ripple and dip on his chest and stomach. The muscles bunch under my touch, and when I get a few inches from his protruding cock, it too seeks my touch.

"I didn't invite you into the shower to—ah fuck."

My hand slips past his eager erection, and I fondle his heavy, potent sack.

"Mia, Jesus," he pants.

His arm goes out to hold some of his weight as he leans to the side, and I take it as my cue to ease his discomfort. My hand circles his cock, the water making it easy to glide up and down the length of him.

"Yeah, baby. Grip it tighter."

My belly flip-flops, a riot of butterflies taking flight inside of me at his command.

"Fuck, that's good," he groans

As if he can't help himself, his hips begin to shift back and forth, seeking a deeper stroke, and I give him exactly what he needs. His fist clenches at his side, and I ache for him to touch me. Reaching down, I lift his hand and urge him to touch my breast and boy does that make all the difference for him. He thickens further in my hand as his fingers pluck and tease my nipple.

"Give me your mouth," he insists, and my head tilts up just in time for his lips to crash against mine.

The arm leaning on the wall reaches behind my back and drags me against him. His tongue invades my mouth as his cock erupts between us. I keep stroking, and pulse after pulse he empties himself onto my skin.

Strong fingers dig into the meat of my ass, and I whimper with my own need.

"Turn around," he rasps against my mouth and then proceeds to chuckle when I spin so fast, I nearly tip over and fall out of the shower.

The humor doesn't last long because he slides his hand between my legs. Finding me slick and needy, it's his turn to groan in my ear.

"Jesus, baby. Why didn't you say something? I would've taken care of you sooner." Two fingers glide through my slickness, teasing my clit before he presses them inside of me.

His dirty talk is new, something I never experienced until now. I always thought it would be silly or it would take me out of the moment and sound ridiculous, but every nasty word, every praise, and every promise of what he plans to do to me makes me need him more.

My knees nearly buckle, but his strong arm wraps around my waist as his other hand works me into a frenzy. My hips buck, jerking uncontrollably as his one hand somehow manages to slide inside of me while still working with expert precision over my clit. He's everywhere at once, and his cock, the very one that just unleashed spurt after spurt of cum on my stomach is thickening at my back like he'll never be sated.

"That's it," he praises when the first tingle hits me low in my belly. "Give it to me."

My core clamps down on his invading fingers, but it's the husky groan so close to my ear that shoots me over the edge. I scream my pleasure, uncaring if the world knows what we're up to in here, but it's over much too soon, and as strong as it is it leaves me still wanting more from him.

"Ryan," I plead.

"Need me, baby?"

I nod my head and not a second later a gentle hand is pressing between my shoulders while the other lifts my leg and positions it on the edge of the bathtub.

"Mia?" I know he's checking with me to make sure this is okay. I know he's terrified to trigger me, but I want this more than I can even find the words for.

"Please," I beg, but the words fade away on a moan as he slides inside of me.

"God dammit," he hisses, and his pleasure makes my body hold him even tighter.

His grip is bruising on my hips as he slides all the way home, but I welcome the tiny bite of pain. It tells me that he's enjoying this as much as I am, and I take pride in that. I want to be able to please him with my body. I don't want him lost in his head or looking at me with disgust because of the things that happened before him.

"That's it. Fuck, baby. Jesus, push back against me."

Standing in his shower, I shift my hips back and fuck myself on his cock, and it's a miracle he doesn't pound me through the wall with how hard we're going at it. His grip on my hips never slips, and as if my orgasm never completely waned, it builds once again.

Releasing one hip, Ryan uses his arm to shift me so I'm standing, and when he angles my head back and crashes his mouth to mine, it'll all over. I swallow my cries as the pulsing begins in my core and a few thrusts later, he's grunting his own release.

He falls free, softening long before I'm ready, but I turn in his arms and smile against his lips. His once aggressive kiss turns soft and searching as his arms circle my waist. He knows exactly what I need and when, and the man is an expert at delivering both the pleasure I want and the comfort I need after.

"How are you so perfect?" I mutter against his lips when we come up for air.

"I'm not." He presses a quick kiss to the tip of my nose before reaching for a bar of soap.

Silently, his hands work the suds over every inch of my body, even the delicate tissues between my legs. His cock begins to thicken again, but I do what he insisted the first time and ignore it. He doesn't seem put out by the lack of attention.

"We need to have a conversation about what we've been doing," he mutters as he angles the showerhead to rinse the soap away.

"Are you having regrets?" I'm able to ask because I'm facing away from him as he rinses my back. I don't know that I'd have the courage to ask the same question if I could see the reaction on his face.

Being physically attracted to someone is not the same as being emotionally attached, and those stupid voices in my head start again.

"We haven't used protection."

A shiver runs down my spine. "I know. I'm clean, surprisingly. The doctors ran a full panel while I was in the hospital."

The memories of what was done to me was enough, and it was a small blessing that I didn't contract an STD.

"I know," he says as he wraps his arms around my waist, pressing his chest to my back. "I'm clean too, but—"

"You're afraid I'll get pregnant?" I swallow thickly and stare at a clump of bubbles as it slowly makes it way down the shower wall.

"Afraid isn't the right word." He presses his lips to my shoulder, pausing for a few long seconds before continuing, "I think it makes me a caveman, but the idea of knocking you up makes me want to fuck my cum into you every day until the double lines show up on the test."

I roll my lips between my teeth to keep from laughing. How did he ever keep all of this shit bottled up inside? It's like some switch was flipped last night, and he went from the perfect gentleman to filthy, and if I'm being honest, completely enticing.

"You want babies?"

"I want babies," he confirms.

"With me?"

"Only you," he says before nipping at my ear.

I turn in his arms and cup his cheek. Sincerity is clear in his beautiful eyes, and I'm thankful for the water cascading down around us because it masks the tears that begin to seep from my eyes. He must see the emotion clouding my eyes because his face falls.

"Please don't break my heart right now," he begs. He tries to take a step back, but I cling to him. "I said too much too soon. I knew I was going to ruin things. Can we just forget I said it?"

I shake my head, before pressing a soft kiss to his jaw.

"You can't take it back, but I can't give you babies right now."

He nods, his strong jaw flexing with the news.

"It'll be another six weeks before my birth control shot wears off."

His eyes widen as if he's having trouble understanding what I'm telling him, but he's a smart man and it doesn't take long for him to work it through in his head.

"Birth control?"

"I asked the doctors for it before I left the hospital. I was terrified I'd be taken again, and I wouldn't survive a pregnancy from one of those—"

He presses his lips to mine, and I squeal, half in joy and half in terror that he's going to drop me when he lifts me up in his arms.

It feels like everything is happening at breakneck speeds, but I think this is perfect for us. We're not going to look back. We're going to plan our future together.

Chapter 35

Scooter

It's been a week, seven blissful days spent in Mia's arms, and it's possible I'm the happiest man in the world.

It hasn't been all sunshine and roses. There has been a day or two where she's a little more withdrawn, but we spent that time quiet in each other's arms, holding each other until the shadows left her eyes and the clouds cleared.

Today she woke up energized and ready to take on the world. I find myself in the living room chatting with Max, watching her in the kitchen with Emmalyn, Khloe, Misty, Jasmine, and Makayla as they throw together a feast for the guys who are scheduled to return any minute.

Her radiant smile fills the air around her, and the other women grin as well, happy that she's come out of her shell a little more each day. They chatter about food and recipes they've tried as they bustle around the large kitchen, and I can't help but picture her in our own kitchen in the house we spoke about building after she confessed that she wanted to build a life and have a family with me.

It's almost the middle of February, mere days from Valentine's Day, and I'm wondering if a diamond ring isn't in her near future. I'd slide a rock on her hand and make her mine all in the same day if things were up to me, but I do my best to keep those thoughts to myself. I don't want to rush things. I don't want her to agree to spend the rest of her life with me one day and then let the shadows creep in the next making her change her mind. I've had patience thus far, and I'll maintain it until she's ready.

The rumble of multiple SUVs marks the return of the Cerberus men, and I head outside to help them with luggage and greet the guys. They're not somber the way we were when we returned from Venezuela. They all have smiles on their faces as they climb out, already talking about the party they want to have later tonight. They need to burn off steam, rid themselves of the residual adrenaline from the job, and I smile, knowing I used to be the same way.

Only currently, I have no steam. Mia woke me this morning with her mouth on my dick. It was the first time her face ventured past my navel, and I won't even embarrass myself by thinking just how fast I exploded from her attention. I returned the favor, not really needing an excuse to put my mouth on her, and that only led to another erection. We haven't used condoms yet, and it's not only because she's on the shot. A long discussion was had after our confessions in the shower. She wants to start a family, and even though it's something I plan to ask Dr. Alverez at our next appointment, I'd be a liar if I said I didn't want that exact same thing.

My only concern is that Mia is trying to replace her pain and abuse with the unyielding love of a child. She has to know that I care for her, even though I haven't confessed those three little words yet.

"Hey, man." Grinch walks up, shakes my hand and slaps me good-heartedly on the back. "How's the vacation going?"

I smile wide as he watches me. I figure he expects me to complain about missing out on the mission, and I do hate that I left them one man down, but I don't have an ounce of regret for the way things turned out. Heading back out and leaving Mia for any length of time will be hell, but I think my head is in the right place. I'm no longer afraid I'm going to lose her, or that I'm going to return to find her gone.

"It's been good, man," I tell him and slap his back in return.

"I can tell by the look on your face that Mia didn't stay gone very long. Is she doing better?"

"She's great, Grinch. Getting better every day."

"We missed you out there this time around," Jinx says as he walks closer. "You gonna make it out the next time around?"

I shrug. I only have a week left of my suspension, but with any luck, I'll be cleared to return to duty. If not, it isn't the end of the world. So long as I have Mia by my side, I could take just about any job and be happy. I'm not saying I want to leave the guys behind, but the loss of Cerberus wouldn't be the end of my world. How could it be when I have the most amazing woman to hold every night?

"Hopefully, man." He claps me on the back as he walks past.

I grab a couple of the rifle cases and follow the rest of them inside. Mia is still in the kitchen, and I know as much as she's healed the last couple of weeks, it's going to take a while before she's completely at ease being in a room with a dozen men.

Emmalyn, Misty, and Khloe greet their men before passing around bottles of beer and letting the guys know that the meal is nearly ready.

Dominic walks in, eyeing his wife like a hungry lion would a raw steak, but after kissing her on the lips and whispering something in her ear that makes her blush, he walks toward me.

"A word?" He turns before I can answer because he knows that I'm going to follow.

Kincaid, Shadow, Kid, Itchy, and Snatch all join us in the conference room. Kid closes the doors, and the loud excitement from being home dulls to a murmur.

"Mia's back," Kincaid says as he walks across the room.

Shadow doesn't go to his computer like he normally would.

"She is," I tell him.

"I'm not going to spend a long time right now discussing all that needs to be discussed because we can get to the later. I miss my wife, and I'm fucking starving, but I just wanted to touch base and see where things are. Where's your head at?"

They all watch me, waiting for me to respond to my president.

"It's in the right place. It's where it should be," I assure all of them.

"You're sure," Dominic asks.

"One hundred percent," I tell them.

"Good," Shadow grunts, and he's the first one to walk toward the door.

"We're debriefing at eleven hundred hours tomorrow. I expect you in here an hour earlier so we can talk," Kincaid says as he walks past me.

And just like that, they're all gone. It feels like a test, and honestly, I don't know if I passed or not, but it's not something I'm going to dwell on right now. Mia and an extravagant buffet meal are waiting just outside of this room, and I plan to enjoy both of them.

The guys are huddled in small groups talking and laughing, and somehow a cold bottle of beer ends up in my hand, and I'm welcomed back into the fray like I didn't royally fuck up three weeks ago. I take what I can get for now because I have no idea what the outcome will be tomorrow.

I chat with Jinx and Grinch as they give me the lowdown on what happened in South Africa. Excitedly, they tell me about the three raids they managed, and even though they complained about being exhausted from hitting the sex-trafficking dens back to back to back in a mission that spanned twenty consecutive hours, they told their stories with grins on their faces. They were able to save the women that were there and eliminated seventeen pieces of shit off the face of the earth.

Exhaustion isn't going to keep these guys from getting loud tonight, and that meant women were coming, and things were going to go down in the living room that weren't for the faint of heart. I mentally begin to make a plan to keep Mia away from seeing things that may trigger her.

But when I look toward the kitchen, I find her watching me. I'm worried that the swirl of activities around her will set her back but she grins at me and winks. I fall a little harder for her knowing that eventually she'll be comfortable around the men I see as brothers. It makes me want to ask Kincaid for a small piece of land across the street. They've already broken ground on Hound and Gigi's house, and I can't help but picture my future starting right across the street as well, but then again I don't know how tomorrow is going to go.

"Dinner is served!" Misty yells from across the room.

Shadow doesn't bother to unwrap himself from her back as she begins to hand out plates to the guys as they line up for food.

Mia steps out of the way, shuffling close to the wall to join me in the living room.

"They act like they don't eat while they're away," she mumbles with a grin when she reaches me.

"Food isn't really on our minds when we're working," I explain.

My eyes track Jasmine and Max as they enter the clubhouse. I'm surprised they weren't here when the guys arrived, but telling from the flush on both their cheeks, they aren't complaining about the delay. When Tug spots them, I see more fire in his eyes than I saw when Dominic laid eyes on his wife. With a quick jerk of Max's head, Tug breaks off from the line of men waiting to eat, and all three of them disappear down the hallway.

My eyes immediately find Dominic's, waiting to see if he's going to go tear into their asses, but he's too wrapped up in something Makala's saying to notice them disappear.

"I think we're going to have to sleep in my room tonight," Mia whispers as she turns and wraps her arms over my shoulders.

She's right, unless those three get it out of their systems enough to head to their apartment, we're going to need a room of separation between us.

She doesn't want her brother to hear what goes on in my room, and I know for a fact she doesn't want to hear her brother going at it with his guy and girl.

I look down at her. "Do you want to eat, or do you want to go to the room?"

She knows what I'm offering. If being out here is too much for her, then we can come back when things die down.

"I'm starving," she says, and it's just more proof that she's healing.

Chapter 36

Mia

I fall to the mattress, breathless with my body tingling from the last hour of exertion.

We spent some time eating and chatting with the guys, but then people I didn't know started showing up, and it was time to get out of there. I was already over-stimulated from helping cook and serve the meal, and the added people was just a little too much. Ryan didn't bat an eye when he saw my eyes darting toward the hall. He simply made an excuse about being tired and led me away.

"You know," I swat my hand at Ryan's chest, "I should be insanely jealous of the women you had before me, but I also kind of want to thank them for letting you perfect that tongue game of yours."

He chuckles but doesn't feed my jealousy. It's just one more thing that makes him perfect.

"Can we have another lesson tomorrow?" I ask when my breathing finally returns to normal.

"I've created a monster," he says with a grin, his head shifting until his face is turned in my direction and our noses are mere inches apart.

"Maybe?" I shrug.

"I don't know how tomorrow is going to go. I have a meeting, and I get the feeling that it's going to determine if I'm going to be allowed to stay with Cerberus or if they're going to give me my walking papers."

"What do you want the outcome to be?" I turn on my side, bending my arms and curling my hands into the center of my chest.

"I want to stay." His eyes search mine as if he's afraid that the confession will change the way I feel about him.

"Then I hope you get to stay."

"You really mean that."

"I do. I think this organization is doing amazing work, and I'm proud that you're a part of it." I mean every word of it.

Without Cerberus, I know I'd be dead. Lots of women would be. They fight every time they leave the clubhouse to eradicate the world from vile, evil men who don't value life, and that's commendable. That's something to be proud of, and if there was a way I could help, I'd step up and do just that.

I want to do something with my life that gives me purpose. I may not be able to fight and serve the way Ryan does, but there has to be things that I'm able to do to help. I make a mental list to ask Emmalyn and Misty tomorrow about local organizations that help women.

"So, when they tell you that you do get to stay—"

"If," he interrupts. "If they let me stay, then yes, we can go shoot tomorrow."

We've had two lessons with the handgun Jasmine offered me weeks ago, and even though it turns out I'm not a terrible shot, I'm not one hundred percent comfortable with it yet either.

Max, Jasmine, and Khloe joined us at the gun range at the back of the property, and even though it was freezing, we stayed and used a case of ammo each before returning to the clubhouse to warm up with hot cocoa and long conversations in the living room.

I had my conversation with Max and it went better than I expected it would. He spoke first, explaining everything that led up to his job with the CIA, and I found myself being more understanding than I thought capable. It seems I've not only healed with my time here, but I've also grown more understanding and empathetic to what others have gone through.

"You're quiet." Ryan brushes his fingers down my cheek, and I give him a small smile.

I haven't had all good days since I returned, but the good definitely outweigh the bad. Today was a good day, filled with laughter and the news that the guys were returning home, but it was also exhausting.

My eyelids flutter when he presses a soft kiss to my forehead.

"Are you sad? Is there something I can do?"

I shake my head. "I'm not sad, promise."

I don't know why these moods come over me. For the most part I'm happy, but then a wave of melancholy slams into my chest, and I can't pinpoint what causes it.

"Was the sex not good enough?" I roll my eyes. "Just moments ago, you were praising my mouth."

"It was amazing." It's always amazing, and we're both insatiable most days, unable to keep our hands to ourselves.

"Talk to me, baby. Tell me what's wrong so I can fix it." He cups my chin when I try to hide my face. "Please don't hide from me. Let me help."

I sigh, not really frustrated at his insistence, but I thought I was fine until he asked if something was wrong.

"Do you ever wake up terrified that everything is going to change? That things are too good right now to be true, like the other shoe is going to drop like an atomic bomb right in the middle of our happiness and ruin everything?"

"Nope." His answer is swift.

"Really?" My eyes search his face, but I don't find a single thing that would make me believe he isn't being truthful.

"I can't think like that. It'll drive me mad." His thumb swirls on my cheek, and I lean in further to his touch. "I mean, I was always worried something bad was going to happen before you came back from Louisiana. Before you left, I would catch myself holding my breath. You were sad every day, but at night I got to hold you and promise that I was there for you, that you were safe with me, and that I would protect you from every bad thing in the world."

I remember those times fondly now, not for the pain and suffering I was going through when they happened.

"But then we'd get out of bed, and you'd distance yourself from me. Then you took off into the freezing cold, and left again after I got back from Venezuela, and both times I thought I was losing you. Both times it felt like my heart was being ripped from my chest, and it didn't matter that it was too soon and didn't make sense. I felt a connection to you the moment I looked down at your broken body in Miami, and that link has only grown exponentially each day. It grew while you were gone, even when I didn't know if I'd ever get you back."

I press my lips to his, but he isn't finished.

"That worry, the fear that you're asking about is what kept me distracted. It made me hate the world and every single evil man in it. I was making it my personal mission to vindicate every woman that had ever been hurt or forced to do what they didn't want to. I let my anger rule my actions, and it could've been so bad. It could've ended not only my life but Jinx's, too, and that's unforgivable. So no, I don't think that the rug is going to be pulled out from under us. I don't let myself imagine scenarios where we aren't together, because I won't ever let that happen. If you run, I chase you. It's that simple. You're literally a part of me, Mia, and I won't survive without you. I know that goes against everything I should be saying. I know that obligates me to you, but fuck if it isn't the truth. There's something between us that I can't explain with words, but it's there, and it's amazing, and it's the strongest thing in the world. I won't give up on that, on us, on you. It's not in me to walk away from that. It's not possible."

Tears burn my eyes, but they aren't the painful kind. They're the ones that come from sheer, utter happiness. He's just said everything I didn't know I needed to hear. I knew he was going to be the one to put me back together, but I didn't have a clue that he would be able to so thoroughly. I thought I'd left broken pieces of me scattered all over the grimy floor in that Miami compound, but somehow, he managed to carry ever sliver out with me when he carried me away from that hell.

"And you want babies?" I ask, my voice cracking at attempting to lighten the mood.

His smile is vibrant. "And I want babies."

"You're absolutely perfect," I whisper.

"Tell my mother that, she still gives me hell about the trouble I caused as a kid."

My smile touches his, and the weight of worry slips away like it wasn't even there to begin with. So long as we're strong and solid, I'm certain we can take on the world.

He looks content and blissfully happy when he pulls away.

"I went to the mall," I tell him. "When I went back home, I felt ten feet tall and bulletproof so I had my dad take me to the mall. He parked close to where I was taken from, and that resiliency that I built up faded the second he turned off the engine. I wasn't strong enough to get out, not even with him by my side, and it gutted me."

"Oh, baby," He presses his lips to my forehead once again, and I allow the comfort, my eyes fluttering closed for a brief moment. "That would be hard for anyone. It doesn't make you less of a survivor because you weren't ready to face that demon yet."

"I went back. Every single day my dad drove me back to the exact same spot. Some days I cried. Some days I grew so angry I thought my dad was going to rush me to the hospital to have me sedated, but every day he took me back. I was finally able to get out of the car. I knew I had to face this on my own, but it comforted me that he was near."

"What happened?" he whispers.

"I went inside and got the lipstick that I was going after the day I was taken." Another tear falls. "When I walked back out with my head held high, I knew I was strong enough to come back for you. I wasn't completely better, but I was put together enough to know that I didn't want to live without you either."

"Baby," he sighs, dragging me across his chest, and kisses me senseless.

Chapter 37

Scooter

"It's going to be fine," Mia assures me as I get dressed for the meeting with Kincaid.

She's naked, still lying in bed, and damn if it wasn't difficult to climb out from under the covers.

"And if it isn't?" I turn to look at her, loving how her eyes rake down the length of my body.

My cock, having a mind of its own and not caring what the future holds so long as it includes Mia Vazquez, begs me to strip naked and get back under the blankets with her.

"We don't even have to worry about that," she says absently, her eyes glued to the strip of skin disappearing as I button up my shirt. "Everything is going to be fine. You'll still be a member of Cerberus when the meeting is over, so worrying about it is pointless."

"I wish I had your optimism," I mutter.

Mia had been my sole focus after she came back from Louisiana, but now I'm forced to reevaluate. I have to be able to split my time and my focus between the woman I can see spending the rest of my life with and my job. It won't be easy, and I know the original members of Cerberus know that, but if they've found a way to balance all aspects of their lives, then I can, too.

"Kiss for good luck?" Mia asks, her eyes finally lifting to mine now that I'm fully dressed.

Leaning forward, I press my lips to hers, but I keep it PG, just a simple brush, because I know going any deeper would make me late and seeing as how my job is already on the line, I don't want to give the guys further reason to hand me my walking papers.

I slip out of the room, closing the door quickly behind me when I see Jinx leaving his room. To say I'm protective over Mia is an understatement.

Jinx and I make small talk as we head into the kitchen and make cups of coffee. He doesn't seem at all nervous about what's about to go down, but I know that has more to do with being uninformed than anything else. Kincaid wouldn't discuss me staying or getting the boot with anyone other than the guys that were included in the brief meeting yesterday. The guys are professional to a fault.

Jinx claps me on the back when I get up from the table to leave, and I take that as his support for wanting me to stay. As I walk to the conference room, I wonder if the guys were asked their opinions about the outcome of today. If I were in Kincaid's shoes, I would've asked everyone how they felt. I need to have these men's backs and keep their safety in mind. If they can't trust me to do that, then I'm useless to the team.

I nod at Kincaid and Shadow as I enter the room, but otherwise keep silent until the other four guys show up. Once the six original members are all in attendance, the conference door closes us in once again.

My palms sweat, but I somehow keep from wiping them down the legs of my jeans.

"Is Mia being here permanent?" Kincaid asks once everyone takes their respective seats at the table.

"She's permanent in my life," I tell him, doing my best not to get defensive. I cleared her coming here before we left Miami, but I didn't consider that the agreement may have an expiration date. "I can find another place for us to stay if it's a problem."

I keep the irritation out of my response, but just barely.

"Her being here isn't a problem. It never was," Dominic says. "Where's your head at?"

I take a minute to reflect before answering because I don't want to seem too hasty, like I've walked in here today with a prepared speech that wouldn't change no matter what I'd been presented with.

"Mia is happy and healthy," I begin. I know the issues I've had have stemmed from her, so keeping her out of this decision is pointless. "Most of her worries are gone, and that calms a lot of issues for me. I'm man enough to speak up from now on if there's conflict."

"You've been seeing Dr. Alverez?" Shadow asks from behind his computer.

"Twice a week. I'm working on convincing Mia to see her as well."

"I think that's a good idea," Kincaid says as he opens a file on the table. "Dr. Alverez doesn't see an issue with you returning to work."

I nod, although I'm surprised. I've practically spilled my guts to the good doctor, and I figured she'd think I was legit crazy from confessing all of the things I've told her.

"I want you back in the field," Kincaid says. "All the guys want you back in the field, but we can't have another incident like what went down in Venezuela. Cerberus is held to a higher standard, and you'll be expected to meet those standards or you're out."

"I understand."

Kincaid nods, and just like that I'm still in and the conversation is over.

The conference room doors swing open, and all the other guys begin filtering in, along with Deacon Black from Blackbridge Security. I keep my head held high as they take their seats. Most of the guys are smiling, but it's clear they partied into the night last night, and this morning's meeting is the last thing they were looking forward to. None of them look at me in sympathy, nor do they have contempt in their eyes. Kincaid told me his expectations, and everyone here has absolute faith that I'll be able to adhere to them.

I do my best to pay attention to the debriefing as they cover what happened in South Africa, but I feel my attention waning already. My thoughts are still back in my room where Mia is still hopefully naked and waiting for me.

An awkward silence fills the room, dragging me from my thoughts, and I look up from my hands for the first time in a while, noticing a stoic woman standing at the head of the table. Every one of the guys gawks at her, and I was so lost in my own head that I don't have a clue what's going on.

"We're a progressive club," Kincaid says. "And I have no doubt that each and every one of you will make sure Rivet feels welcome."

"A woman in the club?" Grinch mumbles beside me. "Never thought I'd see the day."

I slow blink, unsure of how I should respond. I'm not a sexiest man. I spent more than one tour with females in my platoon, but I also know how men are, especially the men of Cerberus who spend their lives saving the fairer sex. We're wired to save them, protect them, and keep them from harm at all costs. How can these guys focus on the targets when they're all going to be worried about her welfare?

"Listen," Rivet says as she takes a step closer, standing more beside Kincaid than behind him. "I know what you're all thinking. 'A woman has no place to be in Cerberus.'"

"That is not what I'm thinking right now," Jinx says with a salacious look in his eyes.

And that's the other problem with this whole situation. These guys' adrenaline runs so hard and so hot, that fucking anything that's willing has always been a way to blow off steam. We can be respectful, but this woman is getting right in the crosshairs of a dozen men who are going to, at some point, want to fuck her. Jinx is already there and it's not even noon.

Kincaid frowns, his eyes narrowing in on Jinx, but Rivet doesn't bat an eye.

"I've fought in combat, and despite the numerous commendations I've received, I've worked my ass off to get here. I don't expect anything to change. I don't want you assholes watching what you say or toning down your personalities in fear of offending me. I don't get offended. I can trash talk and tell filthy jokes with the best of them. I'm here to do a job, and if you fuckers give me half a chance, I'll prove to you that I've earned my spot with this organization."

Shadow coughs to cover a laugh when all of us just continue to stare at her like she's an anomaly.

Kincaid slaps Rivet on the back. "Now that we've got that taken care of, we've been asked to help Blackbridge with an assignment. After the help they've provided us in Venezuela, I figure it's only fair to return the favor."

Deacon Black nods at Kincaid as he rises from his seat and stands in front of the group.

"It's not easy standing up here and admitting that I've failed, but here I am. This mission is more than a little personal for me, and I thought it was in my best interest to come to you guys for help rather than fucking everything up by letting my emotions control the outcome," Deacon explains.

I keep my focus on him as he speaks even though I feel like a jackass for not having the balls to take a step back when I needed to the most. It doesn't feel like a personal affront. Black isn't here to jab at my own shortcomings, but that knowledge doesn't make it sting any less.

"Who are we looking for?" Grinch asks.

A picture flashes on the screen, a blonde with bright blue eyes stares back at us.

"My ex-wife."

Chapter 38

Mia

He gets to stay, which means I get to stay. Right here in the clubhouse where I'm comfortable.

I'm tucked into Ryan's side as he talks with his guys. They partied until the early morning hours when they got home yesterday, and tonight they seem to be doing the same thing. Ryan told me earlier that this is what the clubhouse is like when they get home, and that they were respectful of my being here before.

I smile as I look around the room. There're more than just the Cerberus guys here tonight, and that keeps me close to his side. I've learned to trust these men, but the newcomers cause me concern.

The music is loud, and the drinks are flowing, and for the most part, everyone is just talking, dancing and having a good time. Women in clothes too small for the winter weather outside walk around and chat with all the guys, and I haven't missed the one blond in the corner staring daggers in our direction, but I don't pay her any mind. I'm not certain, but if I had to guess, I imagine that's Kirsty. She doesn't seem happy that I have Ryan's undivided attention, but at least she hasn't come over and tried to start trouble.

Ryan hasn't even bothered to look twice at her, and for that I'm grateful. I know I just shoved myself into his life, but if I trust what he's told me more than once, he's glad I'm here and doesn't want me to go anywhere anytime soon.

"That's not true," Jinx argues. "I don't have a problem with her being here, I just think that it complicates things."

The guys have been discussing Rivet, the newest member of the Cerberus MC.

I don't add my two cents. I'm not a member of this club, but the pretty woman on the other side of the room chatting with Grinch is fierce. She's almost as tall as the other guys in the MC, but there's no mistaking her for anything other than a strong woman. Her all-business short haircut is striking, perfect for her oval face, and more than me, she's getting dirty looks from the visiting women.

If I didn't know how dedicated Ryan was to me, I'd probably worry. He hasn't given me any reason to doubt him, so I won't bother with it. I have enough things to worry about.

"Think we should haze her the same way we would if it was a guy joining us?" Ryan asks with a grin as he brings his beer bottle to his lips.

"I'm not holding back," Jinx says with a playful devious look in his eye. "She said she didn't want us to act differently."

"Can't really give her a gallon of lube and a pocket pussy like we did when Tug came on board."

With a huge smile on my face, I look up at Ryan. "Is that where Kingston got his name?"

Jinx snorts a laugh. "Tug got that name in bootcamp because he disappeared to jack off every chance he got."

Ryan looks down at me, and I'm sure he's checking to see if I'm okay with the direction the conversation has turned. I smile up at him, hoping that he understands that I'm fine.

"She's been in the Marine Corps," I interject. "I'm sure she's seen and heard it all. Oh, who's that?"

We all turn to watch a younger guy walk toward Rivet.

"This ought to be good," Jinx says. "That's Cannon, Shadow's youngest son. He thinks he's God's gift. The boy doesn't know when to quit."

"Come on," Ryan says as he presses his hand to my back, urging me to step closer so we can hear the conversation.

"Hey, baby," Cannon purrs, disrespectfully interrupting the conversation Grinch and Rivet were having.

Rivet frowns at him, but rather than taking him down a notch, she repositions her body to not include Cannon and continues to speak with Grinch.

"Yeah," she says. "Four years was enough for me. The bureaucracy was just too much to re-up."

"Oh," Cannon says as he invades her space. "You were in the military?"

A smile spreads across Grinch's face, but he doesn't say a word. Cannon proceeds to invade her personal space, and I'm finding it a little bit creepy, especially since no one is stepping up to put a stop to the young guy's disrespect.

"Are you a general?" Cannon asks with innuendo lacing his tone.

"Oh, boy," Ryan mutters, but a smile is teasing his lips.

"Cause you just made my private stand at attention."

Rivet glares at him, unimpressed with his ridiculous pickup line.

Grinch coughs into his hand to cover a laugh.

"Wanna help me dishonorably discharge?" Cannon's eyebrows waggle at a comically fast rate, and I find a smile of my own forming on my lips.

This kid is so far out his element with Rivet, but he seems too ignorant to realize she isn't even the slightest bit impressed. It's like a slow-motion train wreck, and as much as I was offended for her just a few moments ago, I still can't take my eyes off of the two of them. Somehow, I just know that this woman can handle herself.

"He can't be serious," I mutter.

"You'd be surprised how many women fall for his shit," Ryan whispers in my ear.

"Well, she's not going to," I assure him.

Cannon inches in closer. "I can stand at attention for hours. Wanna play formation?"

My eyes widen in shock when Rivet's lip twitches. "Surely, she isn't—"

Then Cannon lifts his hand saying, "What do ya say? Are you delta tango foxtrot?" as he trails his finger down her arm.

All humor disappears from her eyes before she grabs his finger and twists it like it's her primary instinct. Cannon squeals like a pig caught in a trap before turning ass over end and crashing to the floor.

Rivet looks down at him like he's nothing more than a nuisance. She spares him the quickest glance before looking back up at Grinch. "So, yeah. Fours years was enough, but I think Cerberus is going to be a good fit."

"And you're going to fit in here just fine," Grinch says as he grins down at Cannon.

The young guy is blinking up at Rivet like he's seeing her for the first time.

Good, I hope he learned his lesson.

"So, I guess now isn't the time to ask if I can put my oorah in your who-ha?"

Both Ryan and Jinx groan at his stupidity, but Rivet just takes a few steps away from him. No one offers to help Cannon up off the floor, and he seems quite content to just watch the woman who put him flat on his back without so much as a grunt.

We back away as well, the entertainment for the evening having lost its shine.

Conversations continue as we mingle, but I never leave Ryan's side. Not only do I love his warmth, but unease grows a little as the party continues and people keep drinking.

When there's a lull in the conversation, Ryan looks down at me, a gentle smile playing on his lips.

"I love you," I blurt.

His eyes sparkle. "Just like that, huh? No fanfare or anything?"

"Just like that." My cheeks heat because I know his friends standing near heard me, but I don't regret telling him how I feel. I've wanted to tell him since I got back. I played it over and over in my head on the way back to New Mexico, but I lost my courage when I saw him standing on the front porch.

"I love you, too."

My heart swells.

"Really?"

"Yes."

His head lowers, and he's all I can focus on. The sounds swirling around us, the people conversing, and the guys chatting over a game of pool all disappear. Ryan and I are the only two people in this room.

The kiss is chaste by most standards, but for me it feels like the beginning of something wonderful.

Three months ago, I was wondering when I was going to die. Right now, I can't wait to begin this new life.

I have a new series coming soon!
Check out One Eighty HERE!

Need more MC in your life?
Give the Ravens Ruin MC a chance!
These bad boys are all about pleasure, self-gratification, and living the good life!
They're NOTING like my Cerberus guys, and this series is a little rougher, a little darker, and filled with enough sexiness to set your kindle on fire!
Start the Ravens Ruin MC Series HERE!

Social Media Links
FB Author Page
FB Author Group
Twitter
Instagram
BookBub
Reader Email Share: HERE

Newsletter

OTHER BOOKS FROM MARIE JAMES

Standalones
Crowd Pleaser
Macon
We Said Forever
More Than a Memory

Westover Prep
One Eighty

Cole Brothers SERIES
Love Me Like That
Teach Me Like That

Hale Series
Coming to Hale
Begging for Hale
Hot as Hale
To Hale and Back
Hale Series Box Set

Cerberus MC
Kincaid: Cerberus MC Book 1
Kid: Cerberus MC Book 2
Shadow: Cerberus MC Book 3
Dominic: Cerberus MC Book 4
Snatch: Cerberus MC Book 5

Ravens Ruin MC

MM Romance

Made in United States
Orlando, FL
26 June 2025

62403502R00115